MICHAEL E WILLS was born on the Isle of Wight and educated at the Priory Boys School and Carisbrooke Grammar. He trained as a teacher at St Peter's College, Saltley, Birmingham, before working at a secondary school in Kent for two years.

After re-training to become a teacher of English as a Foreign Language he worked in Sweden for thirteen years. During this period he wrote several English language teaching books. His teaching career has included time working in rural Sweden, a sojourn that first sparked his now enduring interest in Scandinavian history and culture – an interest that after many years of research, both academic and in the field, led him to write *Finn's Fate* and the sequel novel, *Three Kings – One Throne*.

His interest in teaching children led him to start writing stories for young readers and in 2015 he published the first two of a quartet of novels for 8–13-year-olds in a series called Children of the Chieftain.

Today, Michael works part-time as Ombudsman for English UK, the national association of English language providers. Though a lot of his spare time is spent with grandchildren, he also has a wide range of interests including researching for future books, writing, playing the guitar, carpentry and electronics. He spends at least two months a year sailing his boat which is currently in Scandinavia.

You can find out more and stay up-to-date by visiting his website: www.mic

GW00776689

CHILDREN OF THE CHIEFTAIN: BETRAYED

Also by Michael E Wills

Three Kings – One Throne
The Wessex Turncoat
Finn's Fate

CHILDREN
OF THE CHIEFTAIN
BETRAYED

MICHAEL E WILLS

SilverWood

Published in 2015 by the author using
SilverWood Books Empowered Publishing ®

SilverWood Books Ltd
14 Small Street, Bristol, BS1 1DE, United Kingdom
www.silverwoodbooks.co.uk

ISBN 978-1-78132-401-1 (paperback)
ISBN 978-1-78132-402-8 (ebook)

British Library Cataloguing in Publication Data
A CIP catalogue record for this book is available from
the British Library

Set in Bembo by SilverWood Books
Printed on responsibly sourced paper

Acknowledgements

Thanks are due to the pupils of the Central Academy, Bristol, for the feedback they gave me on an early draft of this novel.

I should also acknowledge the useful comments of Master Oliver Thatcher who, for homework, cheerfully read two versions of the book.

My editor, Agnes Davis, provided an invaluable objective view of the story and made recommendations accordingly.

Thanks too to my wife Barbro who, as ever, cast her eagle-like eye for detail over the various versions of the manuscript.

Michael E Wills
Salisbury
April 2015

Prologue

"Gather round and let me set the scene to tell you how my adventure began."

The old man shifted his position on the stool by the fire and waited for his listeners to get comfortable.

"I was just fifteen, my sister Ingir was a year older than me. Our mother had died two years earlier from the coughing sickness. We lived in the town of Birka on the Isle of Birches. It was a small but busy town which had become wealthy from trading with the whole Viking world and far beyond. But wealth brought trouble and every year raiders tried to grab a share of the town's riches.

"My father, Sten Brightsword, was the chieftain of the town and a fearless warrior. He led a band of men trained to defend the island.

"It was in the ninth month of the year, a time when we did not expect trouble from unwanted visitors, for autumn was upon us and would-be raiders should have returned to their homes for the harvest. Some island fishermen returning home in their boat noticed masts on the other side of a narrow island.

They stopped and tied their boat to a pine tree on the water's edge. One of the fishermen clambered over the grey rocks to look down on the other side of the island, and there he saw a fleet of vessels at anchor in the bay beyond, well hidden from the lookout at Birka. The fishermen recognised the style of the ships as those of the Jomsviking. These were the most ferocious and merciless of Viking warriors. The fishermen hastened home to forewarn their chieftain about the presence of the Jomsviking.

"Having been warned, Father immediately made a plan to take the Jomsviking by surprise. We children watched the whole battle from the top of Lookout Hill, the highest point on the island. From there, in the fine weather, we had a clear view right across the bay in front of the town.

"A trap was set. Very soon, as expected, the Jomsviking fleet appeared. They were heading for the town. Two of our boats were rowed out towards them by crews of six women. The unsuspecting enemy in the ten Jomsviking ships could see the women, but not the twenty warriors who crouched low in the boats. The raiders watched as the women approached them and assumed they were no threat. Their attention thus distracted, the Jomsviking sailors did not notice six longships pulling out of the creek they had just passed. With the help of oars and sail, these island longships quickly caught up with the Jomsviking.

"With a following wind, the crews on two of the longships from Birka lit the seal oil barrels on their decks and then, as their vessels erupted into flames, they leapt over the sides to be picked up by a following boat.

"This lighting of the fire ships was the signal for the women to row forward as fast as they could and for the crouching men to come out of hiding. They would tackle the raiders from the front while the other ships attacked from the rear. The wind pushed the fire ships alongside two of the Jomsviking vessels, spreading the fire and forcing the enemy warriors to leap into the sea. The flames were intense and soon several other ships were on fire.

"The surprise was complete! Many of the unsuspecting raiders had not yet put on their chainmail armour or their helmets when the islanders started to clamber aboard their boats and set about their deadly purpose to defend their island.

"The fighting was fierce, but many of the Jomsviking warriors had been drowned trying to evade the inferno on their boats so the islanders now outnumbered the raiders. With his sword in one hand and an axe in the other, Father led the defenders to attack the enemy flagship. We saw Father wielding his axe and his sword, battling his way to confront the enemy captain on the afterdeck. It was very exciting for us to see, though of course we were frightened that Father might be wounded or worse. After a bitter combat, during which Father got a sword slash to his leg, he defeated the captain and forced him to surrender.

"In victory, Sten, my father, was generous to

his enemy – too generous, it proved. He allowed the survivors to leave in some of their undamaged ships, hoping they would warn others with evil intent that the Isle of Birches was heavily defended and not an easy target for raiders.

"Father's successful defence of the island cost him dear. The wound to his thigh did not heal and eventually red streaks on his leg foretold that his blood had been poisoned. The Shaman tried all his mystical powers to cure him, even calling for the support of Odin, the god of war, but to no avail. Father died a long, slow and painful death.

"The whole island community grieved for the loss of their great leader, the man who had time after time vanquished those who would threaten their lives and livelihoods. But no one grieved as deeply as Ingir and me, for we had lost our father and now we were orphans. Of course we knew how precarious life was for the islanders. We had been prepared by mother since early childhood to expect that death and disaster were an inevitable consequence of life. Nevertheless, it was extremely painful and upsetting for us both to watch as the great man became weaker and weaker every day and we gradually realised that we were going to lose someone we loved so much.

"Now Father was dead, and there was a special ritual for great men. His cremated remains were to be spread on the waters which provided life-giving resources to the community. But those same waters, besides being dangerous in themselves, were also the means by which people with ill-intent might threaten the well-being of the islanders.

"The ritual began as it should. Later, however, things did not go according to plan, but let me start at the beginning…"

Chapter 1

Ritual for a Warrior

The air was still and the surface of the water hardly showed a ripple as two teenagers, Ingir and Ahl, sat motionless, gazing down at the lake from their lofty position.

Ingir wore a long dark-green linen dress on top of which was a white apron. The shoulder straps of the apron were fastened at the front on each side with round silver brooches. Her style of dress betrayed two things: firstly, that this must be a special occasion; secondly, such good quality cloth and the size of the silver brooches showed that there was wealth in her family.

Ahl wore baggy trousers tucked into the top of his boots. To wear clothes which used more cloth than was absolutely necessary was also a sign of wealth. His white shirt was partly covered by a leather waistcoat and around his waist was a thick belt, from which hung a scabbard containing his knife.

Brother and sister sat close together, neither betraying the emotion they felt, knowing that if they did, tears were likely to roll down their cheeks. Tears which might be interpreted as a sign of weakness by the other young people gathered on the rounded rocks on Lookout Hill.

The teenagers waited to see a ceremony that they were too young to take part in. Many others lined the harbourside. Some daring ones, temporarily out of sight of their parents, had found a precarious way onto branches of the birch trees on the land-side of the path which led from the village to the harbour. The low sun was sinking into the western rim of the great lake, and as it did so, the pale pink of the sky gradually gave way to a more serious colour – that of blood.

The situation this evening was special, very special, for only when a chieftain died did all the adults of the settlement attend a spreading of ashes and the dedication of these to the goddess of the lake, Aegir. Every able-bodied person over the age of sixteen had embarked on whatever craft was available to them, to be present at the sacred ceremony. The ashes of the warrior leader, who had led a defence of the island against those who threatened the well-being of his people, would be cast onto the waters of the great lake.

Every fit adult was afloat, except one: the Shaman. He stood on the rocky outcrop by the side of the harbour, a silhouette against the fiery sunset. The outline of his bald head flowed in an unbroken line on both sides of his body to link with the form of his cloak, into a cone shape. He stood absolutely still, like a statue, watching the various craft arranging themselves according to ancient rite. Women and children under eleven years of age were on board simple craft, small fishing boats; warriors rowed the oldest yet still serviceable longships out to form a line some way from the shore on the right side.

Between the women and the young men, some way further out, was a single longship. The finest ship any islander had ever built. The lines of the hull followed the perfection of the classic Viking vessel. Her sail was furled and in the windless evening she floated motionless between the Shaman on the shore and the dying sun. This craft bore the urn with the burnt remains of Sten, the chieftain being honoured.

Sten was not a young man when he died; he had survived over forty winters. He could have lived through more, but for the sword slash which laid him low.

He had gained his position as leader by demonstrating time and again that a well-trained corps of warriors could rout the raids of opportunistic attackers. While Vikings were ferocious and dangerous enough, many of them were merely farmers and fishermen taking the chance to steal from their better-off neighbours. The raid by the Jomsviking had been the most serious, however. They were the most feared and deadly of foes. All of their ships' crews were trained warriors. Every man had taken an oath of allegiance to their leader on the island stronghold of Wollin, in the far south of the land, and they were very well organised fighters. They raided prosperous settlements and plundered them. Not only did they steal everything of value, but they sought 'walking gold' – that is, slaves. Prisoners were a precious commodity and commanded high prices in the slave markets of Miklagård and Dublin.

The sun was now a semi-circle on the horizon and at this time of year, the ninth month, darkness would fall fast. A lantern was lit on the longship; the other boats remained in darkness. The normally noisy watchers on the shore were silent, gazing with rapt attention seawards.

In a short time, as the last sunlight diminished, the power of that single lantern appeared to become greater. On the lake the shimmering image of the single light was dancing towards the shore.

Suddenly the loud, sonorous blast of a horn was heard. It echoed across the lake, but the echo was unnatural, unreal because instead of decreasing in volume, the sound increased. And not only did the sound increase but it multiplied. It was as if the call from the funereal ship was being answered by the spirits of the lake. But these were no spirits, for around the headlands to the north and south of the watchers on the shorelines, the lanterns of five ships appeared from each direction. The hulls of the ships were just discernible in the failing light. As the two flotillas approached the single, stationary longship, horn blowers from all the ships sounded their eerie greeting. All at once the sound stopped and once more the only sound was that of wavelets lapping on the shore. Then there was a call from the land. The voice of an old man, the Shaman, intoned a chant for the dead man. Those who were near enough to the stationary longship could see a man standing in the light of the lantern, pouring the contents of an urn into the waters. The climax of the carefully acted ritual had been reached.

The watchers all knew that the five ships from the north and the five from the south would now turn, extinguish their lanterns and disappear around the headlands, leaving the single longship to row out of sight into the lake, signifying the chieftain's journey to Valhalla. But there was suddenly a clamour on the lake; shouting, screaming and the loud splash of oars. Something was wrong. The watchers on the shore had no idea what was happening on the dark lake, until on several of the ships the lanterns were relit. Ahl and Ingir were on their feet now, straining to understand what had turned the solemn ritual into turmoil.

It soon became apparent that the fleet of mourners was under attack by a superior force. By the light of torches the raiders were forcing the island crews into submission. Unseen by the children, the interlopers' fleet had split into two. Half were engaging the ten longships and the funereal vessel. They had a clear advantage – the island men had not taken their weapons or armour with them for what was to have been a peaceful mission.

The other half of the aggressors had placed themselves between the women's boats and the shore, preventing the small vessels from escaping landwards.

One by one the women and children were seized from their craft and taken prisoner on the larger boats.

The teenagers on the shore were terrified by the knowledge that their parents were being killed or kidnapped. Some started crying, others were struck dumb with fear. Many started to pester Ahl with questions. As the son of the late chieftain, the boy was held in some esteem.

"Who are the raiders?"

"What are they doing?"

"What shall we do?"

As Ahl was considering his answers, he heard the voice of his friend, Ulf, who had been watching from the harbour, but was now, though unseen by Ahl, scrambling over the rocks towards the top of the hill.

"Ahl, Ahl, where are you? Come quickly, quickly…" Ulf stopped in mid-sentence to catch his breath.

"I'm over here, Ulf," said Ahl, needlessly waving his arms in the dark.

"Ahl, the Shaman has sent me…" He stopped again, panting. "He has sent me to bring you all down quickly."

"Why?"

"He is certain the Jomsviking are upon us. They are taking revenge for the defeat your father inflicted on their ships. They have sent a big force."

"The Jomsviking, at this time of year? They would normally have headed south by now."

"Come, come quickly all of you. The Shaman

fears they will take all the survivors from the boats as slaves, and then come to plunder the town."

Ahl needed no more bidding. He shouted to those around him, "We have to hide; we must run to the Shaman for advice."

No one disagreed and the boys and girls scrambled over the rocks and down to the stony path which led to the small town. When they arrived they found the Shaman, a burning torch in his hand, surrounded by all the older children who had been left ashore. The noise was deafening, questions were being shouted, and children were sobbing and arguing.

The Shaman raised his right hand, pointing a finger to the sky. Those watching him fell silent, and those who did not see his signal were quickly admonished by the others.

When he spoke it was almost like a chant, a mystical, musical style of speech.

"Young people of the island, a disaster has befallen us and the forces of evil have overcome our brave men and women. I fear that soon these unspeakable villains will come ashore to steal what we have."

There was some hubbub amongst the listeners as his words added to the terror they all felt.

He waited for quiet, and then resumed.

"The future of our island depends on you, the next generation. The only adults here are those who were unable to go on the boats today, the old and the sick. The Jomsviking will be here soon. They will kill anyone who has no value as a slave. At all costs, for the future of the village, I must prevent you being taken into slavery."

There were some screams and some of the younger children were sobbing loudly.

"I intend to hide you all."

Despite the fear and respect those listening had for this mystical man who was reputed to have direct connection with the world of the spirits, there were several shouts of "How?" and "Where?"

"Some of you may know that trading goods which have to be protected from the weather are stored in the great cavern behind the shrine. I want you all, every one of you, to live in this secret place until I am sure it is safe for you to come out. The cave has a small stream running through it with clean water which you can drink. There are many furs which traders have stored there and you can use them to keep warm. There is also cheese, meat and fruit which have been put there for use in the winter."

Ahl thought for a moment and then dared to call out, "How will we know when it is safe to come out?"

"I will come for you."

"But what if the raiders kill you?"

"Even the Jomsviking respect a man with my position and magical power. They will not harm me."

So saying, he swept his cloak around him and shouted, "There is no time to lose, follow me."

The streets in the town were narrow and so, just two abreast, the young people followed the Shaman towards the shrine.

Chapter 2

Underground

The shrine was a ghastly place for children, and for many adults too. It was dedicated to Odin, the god of war, and Freya, the goddess of fertility of fields, lakes and humans. The wooden statue of Odin was especially frightening. He looked fearsome; his eyes had been carved so that they seemed to be staring at those who stood before him, no matter at what angle. On each shoulder was a raven, Hugin and Munin. It was said that at night, they flew around the world collecting information for Odin, so that he would be wise.

In order to keep Odin and Freya happy, the people of the village left gifts at the shrine. Sometimes these were silver coins and amber jewellery, but often they were in the form of food for the gods. And so, hanging from the branches in front of the shrine, and upon the bench on which the figures of Odin and Freya stood, there were fish, fowl and meat. Much of it had been there for months and the smell of rotten food was awful.

The children were nervous about approaching

the sacred place, but urged on by the sense of near panic which gripped them, they followed the Shaman. As they approached the images of the gods, many started to hesitate.

"Fear not, children, for Hugin and Munin will tell the great gods of the vile work of the Jomsviking and they will avenge your parents. Follow, follow."

Lit only by the torch which the Shaman was carrying, the long procession of children continued. Many were holding hands to help each other as they stumbled on uneven ground. When the old man reached the wooden doors behind the shrine, he stopped and slowly the column of children did so too. He reached under his cloak and produced a key.

"Ahl, hold the torch while I unsecure the door," he said.

By the light of the flame he lifted a heavy log which was on brackets across the door and then thrust the key in the lock and turned it. He grabbed the handle and, with surprising strength, wrenched the door open.

"Ahl, you and Ingir stay here and help me encourage the children to go in. Ulf, take the torch inside and find the lanterns – light them. Hurry, hurry."

As the children arrived at the dark entrance, Ahl and his sister gave them words of encouragement but it was not easy to persuade them to enter. The vault looked frightening and only when Ulf had all the lanterns lit would the remaining children go in.

Eventually, when the last of the young ones had

gone through the doorway, the Shaman came out.

"How can you be sure the Jomsviking will not find us?" asked Ahl.

"Fear not, I will use a pile of logs to hide the door and rearrange the shrine so it is against the door and hiding it. The intruders will not dare search around the holy place."

"And when will we know that we can come out in safety?"

"When the invaders have left and Odin tells me, then I will unlock the door. But Ahl, to more practical things. Deep in the cavern you will find that there is a hole in the roof; you will see the sky and know when it is day and when it is night."

"But what about food and drink?"

"As I have said, there is a plentiful supply of smoked meat, fish and many cheeses which the traders have stored there. As for water, take it upstream for drinking and allow the water downstream for washing and other business."

"Why should I have to remember all these things? I don't wish to care for all these young ones."

"The spirit of your dead father wishes it. Now go, go. I hear the attackers coming to the shore."

He pushed Ahl and his sister through the door and slammed it closed. They stood on the other side and heard the ringing click of the key turning the lock. Then they could hear the Shaman dropping the timbers down on the lock to secure the heavy wooden door. They were sealed inside the cavern.

The noise inside the cave was awful. Some

children were having fun shouting to make echoes. Others were in little groups, gathered around lanterns, trying to comfort each other as they huddled close. Meanwhile, some of the older ones were noisily exploring the traders' stores.

Ingir grabbed Ahl's arm and gasped, "Ahl, what are we going to do about this?"

"What do you mean, 'What are we going to do?' I'm going to look for that meat and cheese the Shaman mentioned and have something to eat."

"But what about all the young ones?"

"They've got big brothers and sisters to look after them haven't they?"

"Not all of them."

Just then there was a loud bang. By the light of a lantern, those nearby could see that two boys had dropped a barrel from a shelf onto the stone floor, and the wooden bands around it had broken. The barrel had split open to reveal a vast quantity of silvery salted herrings. Quickly, a crowd gathered. Those closest started to grab the fish on the ground. Some of the younger children, recovering from their nervousness and fear, joined in the crowd, grabbing the fish. There was another bang and a second barrel split open revealing more fish.

Ahl and Ingir watched as the older children pushed the little ones out of the way and piled up the fish in their arms. Groups of friends made heaps of them by the light of their lanterns and kept others away.

"And who wants cheese?" came a shout from

another part of the store. The owner of the voice started to roll cheeses along the floor of the cave. Some of the children grabbed the cheeses, but the rind was so hard that they could not break into the round shapes.

Then shouting and screaming started up around one lantern as some people tried to steal fish from others. Very soon the same thing happened in another corner.

"Ahl, this is impossible. Soon, everyone will be arguing and fighting."

"There's plenty of food for everyone."

"But there won't be if it gets wasted like this."

"Stop worrying and let's get some for ourselves."

Ahl led his sister over to where a lantern showed a rack from which hung smoked legs of pork and mutton. He took his dagger out to cut a slice. As he tried to do so a voice from behind the rack shouted, "Get away, these are ours, we saw them first."

The owner of the voice pushed two of the hanging legs aside and walked forward. Ahl recognised him as Oleg, the merchant's son.

"You can only have some meat if you can swap other food for it."

"What do you mean? This food is for everyone," reasoned Ahl.

"Oh yes, you stand there with your dagger in your hand and threaten me do you?"

"Oh come on, Oleg, I'm not threatening you, I just wanted a slice of pork."

Ahl put his knife away. He had been given it

by his father when he reached his fifteenth birthday. But with it came a grave responsibility. He, like all fifteen-year-old boys, were warned that such a blade was for peaceful use and that only a coward would use it to settle an argument amongst their own people. Such an act would bring a powerful curse on the perpetrator.

Ahl made to go forward to the hanging meat, but was pushed away by Oleg. He tried again and Oleg raised his fist and said, "You keep off or you will feel my fist."

"Come on, Ahl, we don't need to have the meat," said Ingir, who was behind him.

"No we don't, but Oleg is not going to tell me what to do."

Another figure pushed his way through the curtain of hanging smoked meat. Ruric was well known as a slow thinker, and more famously as a bully.

Ahl pushed Oleg out of the way and moved towards the meat. Ruric grabbed him by his jacket and tried to throw him to the ground. But Ahl carried on and tried to wrench Ruric's hand off his jacket. As he did so, Oleg jumped on his back. All three of them fell on the ground, with Oleg underneath.

Ruric pinned Ahl to the ground while Oleg wriggled free. The bully then sat astride Ahl. He raised his fist to punch, but as he did so he was knocked sideways as Ingir swung a leg of lamb against the side of his head.

Ruric lay on the ground whimpering, "You had no cause to do that, Ingir, I wasn't going to hurt him."

Oleg sat on the rocky floor of the cave complaining, "Look at my knee, I think it's bleeding. It really hurts."

Ahl stood up and in the flickering lamp light, looked disdainfully at the two boys.

"Thanks, Ingir, Father would be proud of you."

"Ahl, this is mad; we have to make some order. Look at the children over there." She pointed to a group of eleven- or twelve-year-olds fighting over some furs. "The most important thing is that we have to be quiet, otherwise we may be heard outside. You must take charge and tell them."

"Why me? I don't want to lead these babies."

"They are not babies. They must understand that we are in danger."

"You do it then."

"Then I will, but I need your help."

Ahl realised he had made a mistake. His sister was older than him, but he was the son of the chieftain. She was just a girl. It was Ingir who was acting like a leader and he was not. He saw now that the children were going wild and that something had to be done.

"What do you want me to do?" he said.

"Find Ulf and some of your friends and get them to bring all the lanterns over here in the middle of the cave. The children will follow, they won't want to be in the dark."

A few minutes later Ahl came back to Ingir with Ulf and some of the other older boys.

"Hurry, go round together and collect the lanterns, tell all the children to come here."

Sure enough, when the older ones grabbed the lanterns, the children followed them to a large area in the centre of the cavern. There were some protests, but where necessary the children were pushed forward to where Ingir was standing. When they all appeared to be in front of her, she said, "Sit down everyone. I know the rock is cold but you won't be sitting there long."

Gradually, everyone did as they had been urged.

"Why are you telling us what to do?" shouted Ruric. There were some voices which mumbled agreement.

"Shut up, Ruric and listen – your life may depend on it," growled Ahl.

The chattering ceased as those listening remembered why they had been brought to this dark place.

"You all know what happened this evening. All the adults have been captured by the Jomsviking. The Shaman fears they will be looking for more slaves, and they can get a good price for children."

"You are exaggerating, Ingir. The Jomsviking will not harm children," said Ragnar. He was one of the older boys, but nobody knew him well. His family had only arrived earlier in the year on their own boat. His father was frequently away on trading voyages.

"We have to do as the Shaman tells us. And

anyway, did they not take the youngest of the children who were with their mothers?" replied Ingir.

"Won't our mothers and fathers be able to escape?" asked one of the younger children.

"Perhaps, but it won't be easy. The Jomsviking have probably bound them all."

"So what will happen to us?" asked another.

"We must stay here until the warriors have left the island. We will be safe here, and if we keep very quiet they will not discover us."

"How long must we stay here then?" shouted Ruric.

"Ruric, don't shout, you fool," said Ulf in a soft voice. "I suggest that anyone making a noise should be gagged."

"I hope that this will not be necessary, but as I said it is very, very important for us to be quiet. Ruric, we don't know how long the invaders will stay. They will be looting all the houses now; they need food for themselves and their captives. And of course they will be looking for silver."

"But Ingir, will they burn the village?" asked one of the smallest girls.

"Perhaps, but don't be afraid, Siv, they can't burn the cave."

"Ingir, I'll tell them about the food," interrupted Ahl. He had become even more conscious of the fact that his sister had assumed greater authority than him.

"No, Ahl, I'll explain what has to be done, and

then you and your friends can say what you think."

"Go on then," said Ahl, regretting that he had not taken charge in the first place.

"We have plenty of food here, but it must be shared fairly and used carefully, in case we have to be here for many days."

"Who is going to arrange that?" asked Oleg.

"Your father is a merchant so you know how to run a shop. You can run a shop here, but everything will be free. First we have to see what we have here. You will need some help. Who will help Oleg?"

Several voices volunteered.

"So I suggest that Oleg picks three helpers and they look to see what food we have."

"What about supper?" shouted Ruric.

There was a chorus of "Shhh!" from the others.

"Ruric, you heard what Ulf said, we will gag you if you can't keep quiet. Since we have so much smoked fish, that will be for supper. We have no cups, so the older ones help the others to use their hats or their cupped hands to get a drink from the stream. We will put two lanterns at the safest drinking place."

"What about sleeping? It's cold here."

"Don't worry, Siv, we have plenty of furs."

"Someone ought to be in charge of giving them out to everyone," added Ahl.

"Yes. Ulf, you have a knife don't you?"

"Yes."

"Can you cut the bundles and, Ingemar, can you help him pass out furs so that everyone has some?"

"Do I have to? I'm tired," said Ingemar. He was a big, strong lad, but he was well known for not being keen on work of any sort.

"Come on, Ingemar, we all have to help," said Ahl.

"Alright then, but they can't all come at once."

"No, let the little ones get their bedding first and then the older ones."

And so it was arranged. Everyone got a share of the fish and then made up their beds. The giggling, sobbing and chatting gradually subsided and eventually the cave was silent apart from the breathing of forty young people. One lantern was kept burning in the meeting place at the centre of the cavern, to provide reassurance if anyone woke during the night.

Chapter 3

An Unwanted Visitor

Just as the Shaman had said, some light entered from a hole high up in the roof at the far end of the cave. At first light some of the children started to stir. Many of them woke to find that what they had thought was a bad dream was reality. They were locked in a cave while their homes were being sacked by an enemy invader. And soon they heard the shouts and curses of the men who were scouring the village to find whatever of value they could.

By light coming in from the hole in the roof, it was now obvious to the residents of the cave what their new home was like. The large cavern had a rough floor, but the path from the locked door to the storage areas was made of wooden boards to allow easier transport of goods. On the right-hand side, when entering the cave, there were rows of wooden shelves stacked with boxes and packing cases of various sizes, and a long rack on which barrels were resting horizontally. It was from these racks that the two fish barrels had been pushed the night before. At the end of the rows of shelves was a large frame on which hung legs of smoked meat. On the left-hand side of the cave, a stream ran in and disappeared through a tunnel at the other end.

Still feeling some resentment about the way his sister had acted the previous evening, Ahl had become determined that he was going to share authority with her. He realised that the chaotic situation of the night before should not be repeated. He was quick to go round to the children as they sat or lay on their beds and tell them that they would soon get some breakfast. He also reminded them to be very quiet.

While he was doing this, Oleg and his helpers, using some boxes, made a bench to put food on. Ahl had lent him his knife and the merchant's son began to cut slices of pork from a leg hanging behind him. He made a high heap of the slices and then cut one of the cheeses in small portions. His helpers broke open a box of apples and put it on the floor at the end of the bench.

Ingir went round organising the breakfast queue and Ulf and some other teenagers made sure that each child got a fair share. Later the older ones joined the excited queue to get their food. Thus, the cave dwellers had their second meal together, sitting around in small groups eating and chatting quietly.

A short while after they had finished their meal it soon became apparent that boredom was setting in. The younger children in particular were finding it difficult to occupy themselves.

"What can we do?"

"Can we go outside?"

They nagged their older brothers and sisters. Some of them started games such as five stones, but it was obvious their stay in the cave was going to be difficult.

Ahl and his friends sat under the roof opening, chatting and gazing at the blue sky overhead. The opening was quite small and partly covered by bushes, which grew around it.

"I am already tired of this place. Can't we try to climb up to the hole so that we can see what is going on outside?" asked Sture. He was a risk taker, much to his parents' concern. He had been one of those who had climbed up into the trees to watch the ritual.

"And how would you do that?" asked Ahl.

"We could put several barrels on top of each other and climb up."

"You might be able to lift one barrel onto a second, but how do you get the third one up?" asked Ahl.

The others laughed. But several of them were already getting bored and were looking for some excitement. They soon found it.

The ground where they were sitting suddenly got darker. The boys looked up and there, peering down at them, was a bearded face framed by long hair which hung towards them as the figure peeped into the hole. He was trying to adjust his eyes to the light, see what was inside.

"Sit still," whispered Ahl, "if we move he might notice us."

Ulf was out of view of the hole in the roof and asked quietly, "What's wrong?"

Very slowly, Ahl raised his hand to his mouth, putting one finger over his lips to indicate that Ulf should be quiet. With the other hand behind his back he waved, indicating that Ulf should quieten the noise of the children. Ulf got up and walked across to where the groups of younger children were sitting and tried to quieten them down. It was quite difficult.

"Ingir, can you get them to be quiet? Something is wrong – Ahl seems to be showing that there is some trouble."

Ingir looked across to where the group of older boys were sitting in the light and noticed Ahl indicating with one hand. He was slowly raising and lowering the palm of his hand and she understood that he was asking for silence. She went round with Ulf and her friend Bodil and managed to stop most of the noise from the young ones by frightening them.

"We are in danger, you must keep quiet, shhh!"

The children started to ask questions, but Ingir held her finger to her mouth and with the other hand pointed to where Ahl and the boys were sitting.

Apart from signalling to Ingir, Ahl and the others tried to be absolutely still, hoping there was too little light coming down into the cave for the man to see them.

Ahl whispered to the others, "They must be searching the village trying to find us or the traders' store."

As he spoke, some small stones fell down from where the man was standing. Then he disappeared. There was relief among the fugitives, but it was short lived. The man's head appeared again, much closer.

"He must be lying on his stomach, trying to get a better view," hissed Sture.

The man leaned further and further down into the hole. Clearly, he had noticed something which interested him. All of a sudden there was a rain of small stones and a loud curse from the bearded warrior as he discovered that he had leaned in too far. He was scrabbling at the undergrowth and overhanging bushes, trying to stop himself from falling. But he couldn't. The boys scattered as the man plummeted to the floor of the cave and landed with a loud thump and a rattle as the war axe on his belt clattered onto the stones.

The other children, who had realised that something bad was happening under the skylight, were all looking in that direction when the unwanted visitor crashed down. There were screams and wails from the spectators. They had been discovered!

Chapter 4

The Body

At first there was a rush as children looked around for somewhere to hide. Ahl and his friends had quickly moved back from the man. They stood for a while looking at the warrior. He lay still on his back, seemingly gazing upwards. He wore trousers tucked into the top of his boots and a long leather waistcoat over his shirt. He had dropped his axe, but still had a long knife, with the handle sticking out of his boot.

Ahl walked over to where Oleg was staring open-mouthed at the scene.

"Give me my knife, Oleg."

"What are you going to do? Are you going to kill him?"

"Just give me the knife."

Ahl put his knife in his belt and joined the friends who had moved a bit closer to the warrior.

"Is he alive?" asked Ragnar.

"I don't know," said Ahl. "Let's have a look."

The four bravest of them slowly approached the man. They stopped when the man suddenly moaned.

But he did not move, and after a few seconds the group moved closer.

"What are we going to do with him?" asked Ulf. "Can we keep him as a prisoner?"

"Have we got anything to tie him up with?" said Ahl.

"I think we should kill him," suggested Sture.

"If we did and then we were discovered, it would not go well for us," said Ahl.

"That's true, but he might die anyway. What would we do with his body?"

The man moved slightly. Everyone jumped back a distance. After a long wait they ventured forward again.

"Ulf, give me your belt. Sture, help me to tie his hands."

Sture and Ahl approached the man. They could see his chest heaving with his breathing. He was definitely alive.

"Ulf, grab his axe and take that knife out of the top of his boot."

Oleg had decided it was too dangerous and kept his distance, but the other three boys crept beside the injured man.

They grabbed his arms and folded them in front of him. Sture held them there while Ahl used the leather strap to bind the warrior's hands together. Only then did Oleg and several others come to look at their bearded prisoner.

The warrior was perhaps twenty-five years old but had already lost most of his teeth. On the right side of his face was a long purple scar.

Ahl suddenly realised that if the man came to, he would see all the children and the place where they were hiding.

"Ulf, get a sack or something to put over his head so that he won't be able to see us."

Ingir stood looking at the motionless form on the ground and said, "What now? What are you going to do with him? We might be here for days; we don't want him here. The children are frightened enough already."

"We've got to get him out of here before he recovers," said Ulf.

"But how? We can't unlock the door. I vote we kill him."

"With his axe, in front of all the little children, Sture? And anyway, as Ahl said, if we are discovered and they find we have killed one of their men, we will be in worse trouble," said Ingir angrily.

Sture was not to be persuaded. "So do you have a better idea?"

"Yes, yes of course. There is a way out of here."

"How do you mean, Ingir?" asked Ahl.

"The stream – the water runs through the tunnel and must eventually run out onto the beach."

"That's a great idea. Only, if we just push him into the water he may drown and sink to the bottom."

"So let's make a boat for him!"

"A boat?"

"Well not a real boat, just something to float him on."

The plotters scattered as the man gave out a groan.

"Do you think he can hear what we are saying?" said Ahl.

"Mmm, perhaps we should be silent, so that if he can hear, he won't know that we are not warriors. Right, from now on we do everything by signs until we are out of his hearing range."

Everyone nodded at Ingir's suggestion. Ahl waved everyone towards where the goods were stored. He whispered, "I think we should do as Ingir said. We need some wood."

"We could take up some of the wooden track in the store," suggested Ulf.

"Or we could use the wood from the broken barrels," said Sture.

"That's a good idea," said Ingir. "Let's find it."

They started hunting around for the bent staves which were part of the barrels, and after a few minutes they had bundles of them under their arms.

"We need something to tie them together with," said Ahl.

"Take the cords which bound up the bundles of furs," advised Ingir. She called out to Oleg to try to find the bindings which they had broken open last night.

After a while they had the materials they needed. They laid the wood in three piles and lashed the separate pieces together to make three bundles. Then, very stealthily, they crept up to where the injured warrior was lying and put them beside him.

There was a bundle beside his feet, one level with his waist and one near his shoulders.

"Right, now we have to lift him onto the bundles of wood," said Ingir.

It was clear that this was going to be very difficult for the teenagers, for the man was obviously heavy. Ahl waved at all the older ones watching to come and help. Some were very nervous, afraid that the man might recover.

Ahl hissed at them, "Come on, we need help!"

Eventually, there were enough volunteers to have two holding each leg, two at his waist and two on each side of the man's shoulders.

"Come on then, lift!" commanded Ahl.

As he did so, the man let out a loud moan. Once more those nearby ran off, as far as possible from the fearsome-looking man.

Ahl waved at his helpers again and desperately tried to reassemble them. Eventually, they summoned up enough courage to try once again to lift the man.

"One, two, three, lift." And they half lifted, half dragged the injured man onto the three piles of wood.

"Now, use the cords to tie him to the wooden floats," said Ingir. Soon the man was lashed to the piles of wood. "Now we have to lift him again and put him into the stream," she said.

"No, no, wait. I have an idea," said Ahl. "If he is found on the beach by the other warriors he might tell them that he found a hole in the ground and saw people underneath. Let's soak him with ale and then anyone finding him will think he is drunk and making up the story."

"Have we got ale?" asked Ulf.

"There must be some in here somewhere. Oleg, did you find any?"

"Yes, there are some small casks. I don't know if it is beer or whatever, but it smells awful."

"Good, bring some over here and pour it over our prisoner."

"Right, we need to get him into the stream."

"No, Ahl, when he is discovered on the beach they will see that he is bound by someone's belt. A belt that's not his," said Bodil.

"Yes, that's right. Then they will understand that there are people still around the village, even if they don't know where. Let's make it look as if the gods have used his belt to tie him " said Ingir.

"Good idea. Ulf, help me get his belt off and tie him with that instead," said Ahl.

The two boys struggled to unthread the Viking's belt and then used it to bind his wrists.

When this was done, the team assembled again. Some took the man's feet while others lifted his back and shoulders. Ahl and Ulf waded into the stream and gradually they dragged the unconscious warrior into the water. The feel of the cold water seemed to revive him and he started to struggle, but he was tied too tightly to his raft to escape. As the current took control he began to drift away into the darkness. As he did so the movement of his body in the water pulled the sack off his head and the last thing the watchers saw was the man wriggling violently, trying to escape from his underground passage to the beach.

"What if he remembers where the hole is?" said Ulf.

"Well, would you believe someone who told you that he fell through a hole in the ground and then the little people in the underworld put him in a raft to escape back to the sea?" said Ingir.

"And especially if the person reeked of drink!" joked Ahl.

They all agreed and the atmosphere in the cave became much more relaxed.

Chapter 5

The Traitor

By the time the injured Jomsviking warrior had been disposed of it was well past midday. The excitement died down and there were complaints from many about being hungry. Once more the older teenagers busied around organising the younger ones to queue for food at the 'shop' bench. Then all the children and their carers gathered around the centre of the cave to eat the food distributed by Oleg and his helpers.

One person did not join the diners. One of the older children took advantage of the distraction of mealtime to try to betray the whereabouts of the fugitives to the enemies of the villagers.

Directly under the skylight, while everyone was eating, a furtive figure tipped some of the seal oil which was used for the lanterns onto broken pieces of the barrels which had been discarded when the warrior was bound to the float. Next, using the flame from one of the lanterns, and unnoticed by the others who were enthusiastically eating their food, the traitor lit the oily wood. A trail of smoke soon wafted up through the hole and into the sky. Having finished his work, the treacherous one joined the diners. The babble of chatter hid the sound of the fire's crackling and so far, the smell of the smoke going up through the hole was not apparent.

It was when one of the younger children went off to get a drink from the stream that the fire was first noticed. She rushed back to her friends and shouted, "There is a fire over by the skylight."

Alarm spread amongst the children and the older ones rushed over to the smoky blaze. Using hats filled with water, they managed to put the fire out. At first the atmosphere calmed, but then questions began to fly. There were shouts of, "Who is the fool who started the fire?", "Did anyone see who did it?", "Why would anyone want to do this?"

Ulf expressed what several of the older children had realised, when he shouted, "Whoever did this was trying to draw attention to the hole in the cave and betray our whereabouts."

Many others angrily agreed.

"But who did it? Who is the traitor in the cave?"

There were choruses of, "Not me!" from around the group of onlookers.

"Shh, I heard something," said Ahl.

The light from the sky suddenly dimmed; clearly there were people gathering around the hole above the children. Everyone moved back from under the hole and once again Ingir and Bodil attempted to get the children to be silent.

The voices of many men could be heard on the

surface, and then a curious wailing started from above.

"That's the Shaman!" whispered Ahl.

"What's he doing?"

"He is chanting, like he does when he communicates with the gods."

The chanting stopped and suddenly, three or four circular loaves of bread, some uncooked fish and a shower of silver coins landed on the floor of the cave.

The light in the cave got brighter.

"They must have moved away," said Ulf.

"But what is happening?" asked Oleg.

"I think the men must have seen the smoke and the Shaman persuaded them it was the ground spirits," said Ingir. "You know, the imps, the goddess Freya's helpers."

"And they thought that Freya must be angry!"

"Yes, of course," said Ahl. "The Jomsviking are very superstitious. The Shaman might have said that the goddess was upset with them for destroying the village."

"And then they made sacrifices to appease Freya!"

Oleg rushed forward, "So now we have some bread!"

"And some silver," said Bodil.

"And some fish we can't cook!" added Ulf.

"If it is fresh, we can eat it raw," said Oleg.

"But we have a traitor to thank for this addition to our larder," said Ahl, and added, "so who is he?"

"Or she."

"That's right, Ingir, it could be a girl."

Suspicion began to grow. Friends looked around and each wondered if the next person might be the one who tried to betray the cave dwellers. Suspicions developed and arguments started, even some scuffles.

Children started telling tales about each other and claiming to have seen each other lighting the fire. Four of the younger children came to Ahl and Ingir to report that they had seen someone acting suspiciously, but each of them seemed to accuse a different person.

"This has got to stop," Ingir said to Ahl. "We have to be able to trust each other if we are going to live together here."

"But we need to know who the guilty person is. He or she might try something else to give our whereabouts away."

"That's true. Surely someone must have seen the person lighting the fire," said Ulf.

"Ulf, Ahl, let's just forget about it and try to keep the peace here until we can be let out."

"No, Ingir, it must be one of the older teenagers. He or she must be punished."

"Punished! What do you intend to do?" Now Ingir was getting angry with the boys.

"We will think of something."

"You will think of something! Look, what you should really be thinking about is why someone would wish to betray us. What reason could there be?"

There was silence while the two friends thought about Ingir's words.

"It must be someone who wants to help the Jomsviking. But why?"

"Could it be that someone has loyalty to a Jomsviking?"

"Yes," said Ahl. "That's it. Who could that be?"

Ahl's question was not answered as suddenly a boom echoed round the cave. Something had been banged on the door, and had done so very hard. All the chatter stopped and eyes were turned to the source of the noise. Then children started to look around to find hiding places; some started crying, others were silent with terror.

Ahl turned to his friends. "Ulf, you have your knife don't you. Sture, get the warrior's axe, and his knife too. Give the knife to Ruric, you take the axe."

There was another bang, though less loud, and another.

"They are moving the timber from the outside of the door," said Ulf.

They waited for Sture to return and then Ahl said, "Is everyone ready?"

There were calls of agreement.

And then he said, "Then let's go to the door and do the best we can to defend ourselves."

The group of young warriors made their way up the wooden path to wait on the inside of the door for the enemy to break in.

Chapter 6

The Shaman's Warning

The defenders stood in a semi-circle inside the door waiting for the Jomsviking warriors to appear. The sound of timber being thrown aside could still be heard and then the loud rattle of a key in the lock. As the key turned the boys were ready, three of them with knives and one with an axe.

The door creaked open and there, with the afternoon light behind him, stood the Shaman. He was completely alone.

The defenders relaxed and dropped their weapons to their sides.

The Shaman held up one hand and in his sing-song voice he said, "Fear not, young ones. The Jomsviking have gone. Their ships are out in the bay. I am very sad to tell you that most regrettably, they have with them all the captives from the village."

Very soon a crowd of children gathered behind the four boys; they had crept out of their hiding places.

"Why did they leave so soon, and so suddenly?" asked Ahl.

"I would like to say that they succumbed to my magical powers and decided this place was too strongly connected with the spirit kingdom. But in reality it seems more worldly factors gave them that impression."

"How do you mean?" Ahl was the only one who dared to converse with the Shaman.

"The Jomsviking have strong bonds of loyalty to each other and a deep belief in the power of the gods to control their destiny. When one of their number emerged floating on a raft, from a journey through the underworld, with stories of hearing the voices of small people, they were very perplexed. Unfortunately for him, but I fancy fortunately for you, he died before he could tell them more."

"And what of the smoke?"

"Ah yes, the smoke, dear children. This was a work of genius in which I was able to play a part. The warriors were about to give up their search for more slaves and valuables when one of them saw a pall of smoke which appeared to come from the ground. He got closer and discovered that indeed it did come from the ground – through a small hole. I was summoned to explain the phenomenon and was happy to tell them that the gods were displeased with what they had done to the village."

"So what did they do?"

"Well, this occurrence, together with the matter of one of their number meeting Freya's imps, was too much for them. They decided to leave, but first they tried to pacify the goddess Freya with sacrifices. I tried to persuade them that she would be happier if they left their prisoners here, but they would not listen. Magic has its limits, even with the superstitious."

"So what is to happen now?"

"First we must house the children. Then I have serious business to attend to with you and your sister."

The Shaman busied about attending to the children in the cave and bringing them out into the sunny afternoon. Much of the village had been destroyed but a few houses remained. The Jomsviking had also spared a few of the old folk of the village who they thought had no value as slaves. The children were allocated homes, either with a big brother or sister or with the elderly survivors.

"We need to feed the children," said Ingir.

"I will suggest to the Shaman that Oleg and his helpers should use the stores and arrange a place where they can all eat together," said Ahl.

Ahl found the Shaman coming out of a house where he had just left some children. He explained to the elderly man how they had rationed supplies in the cave and how Oleg had organised food distribution.

"Be sparing with the food – I will explain why later. When you have made these arrangements come to meet me in my lodge."

"Your house has been spared?"

"Of course. As I explained, the Jomsviking respect a man who can speak with the gods."

Ahl paused and thought for a moment before

heading off to find Oleg. He had never been in the Shaman's lodge, indeed he did not know anyone who had. Mystical signs hung from the walls and door and the house definitely did not look inviting.

As the sun began to set, Ingir and Ahl stood hesitantly by the gate to the Shaman's homestead. Apart from weird markings on the walls, they noticed how threatening the pathway seemed. It was lined on both sides by round boulders. These stones had been painted white and on each one, staring at the fence gate, was a single eye marked out with red ochre.

"Let's come back tomorrow, it's getting late now," said Ahl.

"He asked us to come this evening. Are you afraid?"

"Of course not, don't be stupid."

"Come on, I'll go first."

Ahl did not wish to be shown up by his sister and grabbed the gate at the same time she did. They unhooked the latch and no sooner had they done so than the door of the house opened.

"Come, children, come sit on the bench," said the Shaman, indicating a split log lying on two wooden supports, along the side wall of the house.

The two visitors were both relieved not to be asked to enter the house of the mysterious old man, though neither would admit so to the other. The Shaman sat on the middle of the bench and patted the space on either side of him, inviting the two teenagers to sit down.

"These are terrible times for our community. The village was secure, we had good harvests, fine fishing and there was much wealth generated by the trading."

There was a long pause. The two youngsters were too respectful to break the silence.

He continued, "Now the village is unprotected, our harvest has been looted, we cannot fish for we have no boats, and we have no clever craftsmen to make goods to trade."

There was another silence. It was broken by the clucking of a chicken which appeared from round the back of the house.

"Oh, one chicken escaped the attention of the invaders. Not much to feed forty hungry mouths with."

At the risk of appearing to be insolent, Ahl said, "But we have all the stores in the cave, or what is left of them."

"Yes, what is left of them, it is true, but what is left of them must last us from now until almost this time next year, for there will be no harvest until then."

The three of them sat in the failing light watching the hen scratching the ground for worms.

"She can find food for now, but as the sun rises later each day and its light is extinguished earlier each afternoon the cold will be upon us, and soon thereafter the snow. I have spoken with Aegis, the goddess of the lake. She will provide fine fish for us to smoke and salt, but we cannot get onto the lake to spread our nets. The Jomsviking have destroyed or stolen every craft on the island."

"Can we not buy a boat from a trader when they visit the island?" asked Ahl.

"There will be no more traders visiting us this year, the time is too late. No, we will have to make do with what we have. When the lake freezes we will be able to fish through holes in the ice."

"But what is to become of the village?" Ingir had plucked up the courage to speak.

"Indeed, child, what is to become of the village? It must be rebuilt. But to do that we need timber, we need carpenters, blacksmiths and builders. We have none of these. And of course we need protection. Our brave warriors, the defenders of our community, are as I speak bound hand and foot in the ships of the men who defiled our village."

"If only we had a ship, I could take some of my friends to see if we could rescue them."

The Shaman laughed. "Ahl, you are your father's son; he would have said the same at your age. However, you have never piloted a ship, you have little training as a warrior and there is no ship. The only thing we can hope for is that some of our lost villagers manage to escape before they are sold as slaves."

Suddenly, there was a commotion. Shouts rang out along the lanes of the village. Lanes which had once marked the boundaries of properties, and now surrounded burnt-out buildings. Ulf and another boy, Olaf, ran past the Shaman's lodge. As they ran they just made out three figures sitting on the Shaman's bench in the light of the fading day.

"Ahl, is that you?"

"Yes, Ulf, what's wrong?"

"A ship! A ship has come in! We were walking in the harbour and we saw a lantern out at sea and then we could make out the ship's sails being furled before it was rowed into the harbour."

"The Jomsviking returns?" asked the Shaman.

"I don't know, sir, we just ran."

"The four of you, go into my house and hide. I will go to the harbour."

Now with no hesitation, Ahl and his sister scurried into the mysterious house to find sanctuary, followed by Ulf and Olaf.

Chapter 7

The Young Warriors

Once inside the house, the teenagers looked anxiously around the large room. To one side there was a single candle on a bare table. In the centre of the room was a burning hearth straddled by a tripod with a large metal pot hanging from it. The floor was covered with rushes apart from in one place where there was a large elk hide. Above this hide was a shrine with wooden models of gods. Odin was clearly identifiable, but there were many more. It was difficult to see the wall coverings in the dim light, but the visitors could make out the shapes of runes and pictures of fantasy animals. The creatures seemed to dance as the flames from the fire rose and fell.

Ahl walked over to the small window; the wooden shutter was half open and he craned to look out.

"Can you see anything outside?" asked Ulf.

"No, it is quite dark now. Blow the candle out, it will be easier to see outside."

Ingir blew the candle out and the four of them crowded round the small opening.

"There, over there, coming up the path, there is a light," said Ingir.

"Are we safe here?" asked the other boy, Olaf, the blacksmith's son.

"The Shaman thinks so. Look, there he is, walking with another man who is carrying a lantern."

They heard the chanting voice of the Shaman calling out as the pair reached the gate.

"Come, come, dear children, we have a welcome visitor. Botvid the trader has returned from his voyage on his ship *Orm*, 'The Snake'."

Ahl whispered to the other three, "Isn't that Ragnar's father?"

"Yes, it surely is," said Ulf.

The door opened and the old man came in followed by the new visitor, who held up the lantern to light their entrance.

"But you are in darkness, my children. Do my keepers frighten you?"

"Your keepers?" asked Ahl.

"Yes, the spirits of the house who guide me in my work. They are strong – do you feel them?"

There was an eerie silence while the visitors considered whether they felt a spiritual presence.

"I fear that none of you are favoured with my gifts." He paused and then said, "Botvid, listen to the children's tale."

Ahl spoke, "The Jomsviking have taken all the women and young children along with the men, but Ragnar, your son, is safe. He was with us in the cave where we hid."

"Is that how you avoided being taken by the invaders?"

"Yes, we hid for two days, until the Shaman told us it was safe to come out."

"Very cunning, well done. So what will you do now?"

"The Shaman has advised us that the winter will be difficult, unless we can get boats to go fishing."

"This is true."

"We would like to try to rescue the captives before they are sold as slaves, but we have no boats."

"You have now, I have a good ship."

The Shaman interrupted, "But these are only children, they know nothing of danger and fighting."

"Quite so, but this is the only chance for the villagers to be rescued."

"I must protest. We are talking about the most terrible of foes, the Jomsviking. What chance would these children have against them?"

"Surprise. The villains will not be expecting anyone to dare to challenge their power."

"Nonsense. They will be very alert, guarding their prisoners; they are valuable to them. I insist the young ones must stay here."

"To starve, while their parents are sold to Turkish merchants in the market place in Miklagård?"

There was a long silence. The teenagers were stunned to hear the Shaman's authority challenged in this way.

The old man's voice was weak and betrayed his

anguish when he asked, "Botvid, what do you have in mind?"

The ship owner hesitated for a few seconds. Then he said, "The invaders will need to take the slaves to the market in Dublin, or probably Novgorod where they will get a better price, as soon as possible. They won't want to feed them through the winter. I am sure that since the prisoners will be bound the Jomsviking will only need a small number of men to guard them. If I can take twenty of the strongest and best young ones from the village I am sure we could rescue the captives."

"In my lifetime I have seen many awful things. But nothing, nothing equates with this loss of our men, women and young children. No, no, this is a terrible thing. To lose all the teenagers as well would mean the end of the community. Ahl, Ingir, tell him I am right."

There was an awkward silence. Then Ahl plucked up enough courage to say, "If twenty of us go with Botvid, there will still be almost twenty children left. Should anything awful happen to us, the community would endure through these children."

It was obvious from these words that Ahl was in favour of Botvid's scheme. His position was strengthened when Ingir said, "It is what our father would have wanted us to do."

The lantern light accentuated the Shaman's sad and perplexed face. He drew a deep breath and then slowly made a pronouncement.

"So be it, I cannot stop you. But if disaster should befall you, remember, I counselled against the idea. Now, will you leave my house for I must speak with the gods to request the most favourable outcome to your venture."

The teenagers nodded respectfully to the old man and then followed Botvid out of the house into the dark garden. When they had found their way through the garden gate, Botvid said to them, "Meet me at my boat after dawn tomorrow morning and bring with you a crew – at least twenty of you altogether. Make sure that my son is one of the crew."

"What about weapons?" asked Ahl.

"Ah yes, do you have any?"

"Well, some of us have knives, and there are wood axes in some of the houses."

"Good, bring what you can. Make sure that all the children have warm clothes and oilskins if possible. Then we must persuade the Shaman to let us have provisions from the cavern store."

"Till tomorrow then," said Ahl.

"Yes, till tomorrow," answered Botvid as he hurried off with the lantern, leaving the four teenagers to find their temporary homes in the dark. When they parted, Ahl said, "Ulf, consider who we should take with us. We want the strongest and most reliable boys."

"Boys! Oh no, some girls are going too," protested Ingir. "You and your friends may be strongest, but you need the brains of women to help you plan how you are going to rescue the captives."

"This is not a job for girls," said Ulf.

"Do I have to remind you that one of the greatest and strongest of the gods is a woman? Girls can tolerate hardship and pain far better than boys can."

Ahl did not want to fall out with his sister; she was now his only relative. He drew a deep breath and then said, "Alright, you can bring Bodil and two others. Ulf, that means we need sixteen boys."

"Yes, with you, me, Ragnar, Olaf and Sture, we need eleven more. What about Oleg and Ruric?"

"Um… Ruric is a bully, but he is a big strong lad. Yes, we will take him."

"We can go round the houses at first light and choose another nine."

"Agreed. Ingir, you had better consider which girls you want to take."

"I already have. I will ask Anneka and Gunhild."

"Anneka the butcher's daughter? Isn't she a bit young?"

"Yes, but have you seen how strong she is? I have seen her helping her father slaughter sheep. He works her very hard and she never complains."

"Alright, your choice. Ulf, Olaf, come to our house at first light to make our final list of young warriors."

Chapter 8

Orm Sets Sail

The next morning it soon became apparent that Ahl had been very optimistic about the young army. Many of the teenagers they had chosen to go with them were frightened and refused. The prospect of a sea voyage and confronting the feared Jomsviking was too much for them. Some of the boys they had to take were not the ones that Ahl and Ulf would have chosen. They even had to take Ingemar, despite his reputation for laziness. He obviously thought there would be less work to do on a voyage than staying in the village and rebuilding houses. Indeed, it became so difficult to find enough boys to volunteer that eventually Ahl agreed to let Ingir take four friends instead of three. She chose Birgit, the baker's daughter.

And so it was that much later than intended, fifteen boys and five girls filed down the path to the harbour. Each of them struggled to carry cloaks and such wet weather clothing as they were able to find. Several of them also carried long-handled axes and one boy had found a spear.

When they arrived at the jetty, Botvid was waiting for them. He showed his annoyance at their lateness by greeting the group saying, "Half the day has gone, where you have been?"

Ahl ignored his remark and said, "Have you asked the Shaman about provisions for the journey?"

"Yes, he has agreed to let us take a barrel of salt fish, some cheeses and rye flour, as well as a couple of boxes of apples."

Ahl found himself looking carefully at Botvid. Apart from in the gloom of the Shaman's house, Ahl had never seen the man close up before. He was a burly man with straggly black hair which reached his shoulders. His brown eyes had a sinister hint and in the middle of his face, which was partly covered by a patchy grey beard, his mouth seemed to have a perpetual sneer with one side higher than the other. The higher side betrayed several yellowed teeth. Botvid glanced at Ragnar, his son, and raised his hand slightly in salutation to him.

Several of the teenagers were very nervous about their proposed expedition and Ahl sensed that the appearance of the ship's captain did nothing to ease their hesitancy. He had to do something to reassure his friends. He quickly decided that the best thing would be for him to say some words of encouragement. He turned and addressed the group.

"We are on an important mission. We are all young, but we are going to rescue our families and win great fame and admiration as warriors. Now, take your belongings onto the ship and then we will all go to collect provisions for the journey."

Botvid was annoyed that Ahl had taken the initiative, but said nothing. He only added, "Put your belongings in the central hold and we will decide which your places are later."

The youngsters walked up the gangplank to deposit their clothes and weapons as instructed. Ahl looked at the ship. It was a typical Viking knar, a sturdy trading vessel, though a large one. He judged it to be twenty paces long and perhaps up to five paces across. The bow and the stern ended in a point, the front higher than the back. There were eight holes for oars on each side, many fewer than on a longship, as on the knar the main means of propulsion was the large sail which was at the moment furled on a long yard arm. In the centre of the ship there was a large open cargo hold.

Sitting on a bench in the stern were two men. Ahl was surprised to see them – he had not realised that Botvid would have his own crew with him. Neither of the men helped the teenagers to unload their belongings, they just watched the newcomers and occasionally glanced knowingly at the captain. One of them, who had no hair at all, was dressed in typical sailor fashion with a tunic and his baggy trousers tucked into his boots. He carried a long knife in a scabbard hanging from his belt. The other, a smaller man with unusual features, had a kind of short cloak and tattered breeches.

Botvid noticed Ahl looking at the two men. He walked over to Ahl and said, "I will take my crew with us. We need to have some experienced help. The bald fellow is Grim, the thin one is my slave. We call him Slav, he comes from the south of the land of the Rus, and he doesn't speak much of our language."

Ahl looked at the men again and began to feel some unease about them. His thoughts were interrupted by Ingir, who grabbed his arm and pulled him aside, out of hearing of the others. She said, "Have you seen those two men sitting at the stern?"

"Yes, they are Botvid's crew; the thin one is a slave."

"They both look as if they would slit our throats for a bit of salt herring."

"Well, Ingir, we don't have much choice. If we are to try to rescue our island folk we have to trust these men."

"And another thing, if Botvid has just returned from a trading journey, where are the goods he has traded?"

"Ingir, stop worrying. This is our best chance to catch up with the kidnappers."

"I think we should be very careful, these men look like—"

Their conversation was interrupted by Botvid, who shouted across to the pair, "Come on, you two, we have to hurry up and get the provisions aboard."

"Of course, Captain," Ahl responded, and turning to the teenagers who had gathered in a group by the side of the ship, he said, "I think that the Shaman will be waiting for us at the cave; he will show us what we can take as provisions. Come on, let's go."

"Ahl, leave Ragnar here, I need him to help me fill up the water barrel."

The chieftain's son was puzzled by the request. Surely the two crew would be able to help with such preparations? He paused for a moment, about to disagree, and then reminded himself that Botvid was the captain of the ship and they needed his help.

"Alright, Ragnar, you stay with your father."

And so, nineteen of the teenagers filed along the path towards the cave. The Shaman was indeed waiting and supervised the allocation of the goods which they placed in wooden tubs.

When they were ready to leave, he turned to face the group and said, "Dear children, it is indeed a dangerous mission on which you embark, but fear not, the gods are with you, you have my assurance. When you return with the captives there will be great rejoicing and you will have won honour as warriors. I appoint Ahl as your leader and to signify this, here is the chieftain's sword, which was once wielded by his father; he named it *Defender*."

He pulled the sword out of the scabbard and handed it to Ahl. It was magnificently decorated the whole length of the blade. The handle was bound with red leather and the silver pommel at the end of the handle was made in the shape of a fist.

"Carry this to the ship and wear it when danger threatens. May Odin and Thor be with you."

Ahl was shocked by the honour bestowed upon

him and, for a moment, speechless. The silence was filled by Ingir, who shouted, "Get into pairs and carry a tub each between you."

Ahl took the head of the procession while the others formed up in pairs with their loads. Ingir was last in line and found herself alone, without someone to help with her tub. She called out to Ahl, "Aren't there nineteen of us? Ragnar stayed on the boat didn't he?"

"Yes, that's right," said Sture, who was in front of her.

"Then if Ahl is at the front carrying the sword, there should be nine pairs of people to carry the boxes. Someone is missing!"

There was a babble of talk amongst all the teenagers and Ahl walked back to try to work out who was missing. Things got somewhat chaotic as everyone tried to identify which person was not in the line. Then Oleg called out, "It's Ingemar, yes he's the one. Where is the lazy scoundrel?"

"Yes, it must be Ingemar," said Ingir.

"He must have run away," commented Ahl.

"He is too lazy to run anywhere," Sture quipped.

"Did anyone see him at the ship?" asked Ahl.

Several voices called out to confirm that he had been there.

"I remember he was carrying a large black cloak with a white trim and an axe," said Bodil.

"Well, let's get back to the harbour and see if we can find him. I'll put the sword on my belt and help Ingir. Off we go."

The party made their way back to the ship. When they got there they found Botvid and the three others still filling up the barrel from the stream some distance away. The captain called out, "Leave the tubs by the side of the ship, we are almost ready here."

Ahl climbed onto the ship to see if there was any sign of Ingemar's cloak. He did not need to look far, for the cloak was indeed there on top of the pile of other coats and cloaks. Ahl noticed a shape under the cloak. He slowly pulled it back, and there, fast asleep, was Ingemar.

Ingemar was a big boy, but not heavy enough to stop Ahl grabbing his tunic and lifting him. He shook the sleeper to wake him.

"You lazy villain, you sleep while everyone else works! You will pay for this. I will see to it that you get all the hardest jobs from now on."

There were shouts of agreement and some cursing from the other teenagers as they expressed their anger at the boy.

Ingemar sat up and blinked at the light; he rubbed his eyes and then said quietly to Ahl, "You may come to change your mind when I tell you what I have heard."

"I don't care what you have heard, get off the boat and help the others with the loading."

"But wait, I have something to tell you – it's important."

"Important or not it will have to wait until we have set sail." Ahl gave Ingemar a push towards the others who were waiting by the pile of tubs.

Botvid, Grim and Slav lifted the water barrel onto the foredeck and then the captain supervised the loading of the tubs. After this he assembled the young warriors on the quay and said, "This ship has eight thwarts, these are the benches you sit on for rowing. You row in pairs, so sixteen of you will have your own places for rowing where you will also eat and sleep. Put your belongings and waterproofs under the thwart."

"But there are twenty of us," called Oleg.

"Yes, that is true. Four of the girls will have their place on the foredeck. They will do the cooking and pass water to the rowers."

This was too much for Ingir. She shouted, "We girls can row as well as the boys, why should we do all the cooking?"

"Because I say so and I am the captain!" growled an irritated Botvid.

"Unless we can all share the rowing and cooking the girls will not go."

There were calls of agreement from the other four girls. Ahl knew how stubborn his sister could be and he leant forward to Botvid and said, "I am sure the boys won't mind if the girls row too."

Botvid glared at Ahl and then the glare eased slowly into his lopsided smile.

"Alright, alright. We will work out some kind of rota so that everyone gets to share all the different tasks. But the girls can still keep their things under the foredeck."

There were sounds of general agreement amongst the teenagers. Ahl breathed a sigh of relief and asked, "Does it matter who sits where?"

"No, but I want Ragnar to sit in the row nearest the stern. My place is by the steering oar and I want to teach him to steer the ship. And you too should sit near me, Ahl, so that we can discuss our plans."

"Can you tell us where we are going?" asked Ahl.

"Yes, we are going around the north of the island and then we go east. The Jomsviking will most likely be taking their captives to the nearest slave market which is in Novgorod, on the route to Miklagård. Winter will be on us soon and they will not want to have to feed their prisoners all through the long cold season."

"Do you think we will catch up with them?"

"Of course, or I wouldn't have taken you all on the *Orm*."

Ahl looked round at his friends and told them to take their places on the ship. All of them at some time had rowed before, so there was no need for any instruction. Slav was standing on the quay at the bow holding the mooring line and Grim stood at the stern. The ship was facing into the light wind and when Botvid gave the order, Slav pushed the bow off the quay and jumped aboard. The wind turned the vessel on its stern. Grim gave a push and he too jumped aboard.

"Ready with the oars!" called the captain. He looked along the boat to see if all the oars were in position through the ports.

"Ready, follow my count. One," he shouted loudly, and then quietly, "two, three, four." Then again, "One, two, three, four."

Gradually, after an uneven start and much banging together of oars, the rowers got into rhythm. They continued rowing until the vessel had reached the northern tip of the island and then Botvid called out, "When I give the order, everyone stop rowing."

There were comments of relief from around the ship. The oars were heavy and the teenagers were unused to this kind of work. Before Botvid stopped them rowing, the two crew had come forward and started hoisting the sail. When it was halfway up, Botvid shouted, "Stop rowing! Bring in your oars."

The rowers wearily dragged in their oars and stowed them. Some just leant forward to rest, others started chatting, a few started moving around the ship. One of these was Ingemar. He came waddling along the rolling deck towards Ahl. When he reached him, he nervously looked at Botvid and Ragnar to see that he was not observed and whispered, "Ahl, I really must talk to you. It is very important."

"Well, tell me then."

"Shh, not here. Come forward to my thwart, Ingir might want to hear too."

Ahl called to Ingir and together they made their way to where Ingemar was waiting for them.

"Well, Ingemar, what is it?"

He looked nervously around him and said, "It is a matter of life or death – your life or death."

Chapter 9

The Conspiracy

Ingir and Ahl squeezed up close to Ingemar on his thwart and glanced around to make sure that no one else was listening.

Ahl leant forward and turning to face Ingemar, said quietly, "Tell us then, what did you hear?"

"Well, I was tired this morning so I hid under the clothes and tried to get some sleep, but I heard Botvid call Ragnar and then the two of them stood near the hold talking. I can tell you, I could hear every word. It was impossible to sleep."

Ahl was getting irritated with Ingemar; he said, "Yes, yes, but what did they say?"

"It was Ragnar who spoke first. Let me see, he said something like, 'Sorry I couldn't let you know where we were hiding – I tried. I lit a fire under the hole in the roof in the hope that someone would see the smoke.'"

"So it was Ragnar! He was the one who tried to betray us. Just wait, I will throw him to the fishes," threatened Ahl.

Ingir grabbed Ahl's wrist and whispered, "Steady,

Ahl. Calm down, we must be very careful not to upset the others and we must definitely not let Ragnar know we have identified him as the traitor."

"Why not? He is despicable."

"Because, well, because of what I am going to tell you next," said Ingemar.

"Why, what else did he say?"

"It's not what he said, but what his father said."

Ingir tried to calm her impetuous brother and asked, "What more did you hear, Ingemar?"

Just then the captain's voice boomed out, "Sit down, we can't have you all wandering about on the ship. Stay in your places. Ahl, can you make sure that people take it in turns to stretch their legs, then come to the stern to see me, we have plans to make."

Ahl looked at Ingemar and said quietly, "I'll come back to see you when I have had a talk with Botvid."

Ingir grabbed Ahl's sleeve and said, "Not a word about what Ingemar has told us!"

"No, I think you are right. We should keep this to ourselves for the moment."

Ahl made his way to the stern and stood next to Botvid.

"What were you three conferring about?" enquired the captain.

"Oh, just talking about the um, the voyage."

Botvid was silent for a moment and then said, "The wind is from the west, which is good for us. Before dark we will take the ship into a sheltered bay I know and anchor from the stern. We will tie the bow to a tree. The crew can go ashore and we can make a fire to cook our food on. This is what we will do each evening until we get out into the great sea."

"Won't we be wasting time? Shouldn't we sail at night?"

"No one sails in the dark in these waters; there are rocks and shoals just waiting for the unwary seaman to make a mistake."

"When will we be stopping then?"

"Just before dark. You decide who will cook this evening and send some of the others to get firewood. We will have hot porridge and salt fish each evening and cold porridge and salt fish in the morning. We will eat the cheese and apples in the middle of the day. We must be careful not to use too much food, it may have to last a long time."

"I will ask Oleg to give out the supplies to the cooks each day."

"No you won't. I will decide how we should ration the food. Send your cooks to me when we have moored and you have chosen them."

There was a change in tone from the captain. Now that they were at sea, he was gruffer and used a more demanding voice. Ahl was unhappy about this, but tried to tell himself that this was something he would have to put up with. Botvid's ship was indispensable if they were to find the captives. He refrained from reacting and moved over to Ingir to explain what Botvid had instructed him to do.

"I am sure that none of the boys even know how to make porridge," was her reaction.

"Then if you want to share the jobs between the girls and the boys, you will have to teach them."

"Then I will. You choose two boys to help Bodil and me this evening. Then those two can teach two others tomorrow and so on each day."

Their conversation was interrupted by a shout from the captain: "Standby to lower the sail. Get your oars ready. Ragnar and Ulf, help Grim with the sail."

Ahl had been preoccupied with making the arrangements as instructed and he had not noticed that they were approaching a headland on an island. He hurried to his rowing place and there was much bustle as the rowers got their oars ready. The captain pulled on his steering oar and the ship changed direction. As they rounded the headland, the sail was lowered and they found themselves in much flatter water in the lee of the rocks and trees. Botvid called an instruction to Slav in the stern of the vessel and he started to uncoil a line which was attached to a rope basket containing a boulder.

"Steady now, row slowly," the helmsman, Botvid, shouted loudly. "You girls in the bow, now's your chance to show what you can do! Let's see if they are worth their salt, shall we, Grim?"

The two men laughed. "Two of you jump off the bow when we get right up to those rocks. When you are ashore, a third one throw them that line which is coiled up on the foredeck."

The rowers slowly propelled the ship towards the shore. When they were roughly three boat-lengths out, Botvid left the steering oar and helped Slav lift the boulder which was to act as their anchor. They threw it over the stern and it splashed noisily into the sea.

"Keep rowing slowly until I tell you to stop."

There was a quiet pause while the rowers did as they were commanded. Anneka and Gunhild stood balanced, one on each side of the high prow of the ship, waiting for their chance to jump onto the huge round rocks they were approaching. Ingir had the coil of rope in her hand.

"Stop! Ship oars!" Botvid's instructions were immediately obeyed and the vessel quietly glided forward, losing speed all the while. It had all but stopped when the girls jumped. The rowers, with their backs to the bow and the captain right at the stern, could not see what happened, but the scream and the splash foretold that at least one of the girls had jumped too soon or missed their footing on the rock.

There was an audible mass intake of breath from the rowers when they realised that something had gone wrong. But a significantly louder noise was the cursing of the captain.

"You damned fools, you jumped too soon. Ingir, can you see them?"

Ingir was bending over the bow. She was holding out the end of the rope to Anneka who was in the deep water. She turned round and shouted, "Anneka has fallen into the sea."

"Ingir, what the hell are you doing? Let the girl drown, we have to control the boat."

Several of the boys ran to the bow to help Anneka, who was holding onto the end of the rope, back into the ship.

Meanwhile, Gunhild had scrambled onto the rocks and was waiting for the line to be thrown to her. Although the ship was in the lee of the land, there was enough breeze to start driving it backwards. Ingir threw the rope to Gunhild, but now the distance was too great and after several tries, it was clear that it was not going to be possible to get the line ashore.

"You blasted idiots, you imbeciles, can't you do anything right?" The captain was beside himself with rage. "We should not have taken females on a ship, it was bound to turn out badly. Man your damned oars."

Several of the boys were at the bow, commiserating with Anneka.

"I said man the oars. Are you deaf?"

They all scrambled to their positions. The captain shouted further instructions, first for the rowers on the starboard side only to row, and then all together, until eventually *Orm* was once more heading in towards the shore and the stranded Gunhild. The line was thrown to her; she took it round a tree and threw the end back to Ingir to secure the ship.

Botvid did not comment further on the berthing manoeuvre, but at the first opportunity and out of the captain's hearing, several of the boys commented to each other and to Ahl about the display of foul temper they had just witnessed. On the shore, Ingir took Ahl aside and said, "This man is a brute – are we really going to put up with his cruelty?"

"I don't see that we have much choice. We need his boat, and only he knows how to find the Jomsviking. How is Anneka?"

"Cold and very frightened. Fortunately, she could swim! Not all of the crew can. I can and so can Anneka, but not many of the others. That despicable man actually suggested that we should let her drown just to save his wretched boat."

Their conversation was interrupted by a call from the captain, who was sitting on the ship: "Who is doing the cooking tonight?"

Ahl called back, "Ingir and Bodil are working with Oleg and Ulf, and the girls are going to teach the boys to cook."

"Well get on with it, we are hungry."

It was while they were sitting round the fire, after the meal, that Ingemar crept up behind the brother and sister. He whispered, "I've got to talk to you, I didn't finish telling you what I heard."

"Oh yes," said Ahl, "let's go over there, where we can't be heard."

The trio shifted away from the fire and sat on some boulders.

"Well, Ingemar, what is it?"

The boy was quite excited and started speaking very quickly. "You know I told you about what Ragnar said he did in the cave, and what his father said?"

"Slow down, Ingemar, let me see if I have understood this properly," said Ingir. "Ragnar was trying to let his father know where we were hiding. That must mean that his father was with the Jomsviking…"

"Then he must be one of them," interrupted Ahl.

"Yes, yes that is what I am trying to tell you. This whole thing is a trick."

"What do you mean a trick?"

"Ingir, don't you see? They could not find us on the island, but they knew we were there. So they went away, and when it was safe we came out. They sent Botvid with his boat to offer us a chance to recover our parents…"

"And then of course Botvid knew that by giving me the chance to choose the best crew for the voyage, I would be choosing those who had most value on the voyage and also best value in the slave market. Oh by the gods, we have been fooled."

Ingir broke in, "All he has to do is to let us catch up with the Jomsviking. He will pretend to be helping us free the captives, but in reality he will just hand us over."

"That is what I was going to tell you. That is what he told Ragnar while I was hiding. But it is worse. He knows that you may make trouble for him and he told Ragnar that if you do, he and Grim will throw the two of you into the sea later in the voyage. He also said he wants that sword you brought on board."

All three of them were silent while they considered the real consequence of the voyage they had embarked on. After what seemed like several minutes, but was in fact only several seconds, Ahl said, "Thanks, Ingemar. Look, please don't mention this to anyone until we have decided what is to be done. Go back to the others while Ingir and I have a think."

When he had gone Ahl whispered to Ingir, "There are twenty of us – we can overpower the three of them easily."

"No, Ahl. As you have pointed out to me, we need Botvid and his crew to sail this ship and to lead us to the Jomsviking."

"So what do we do?"

"We have to make a plan. Somehow we have to get Botvid to lead us to the Jomsviking without giving him the chance to hand us over to them."

"Or throw us into the sea!"

Chapter 10

Subterfuge

All through the next day's voyage Ahl and Ingir were thinking individually about how to deal with the situation in which they found themselves. It was not until after supper that they had a chance to talk in private.

"Ahl, obviously we have to do all we can to prevent the teenagers being taken captive, but our objective is to get the release of all the islanders."

"Yes, you are right. We must confront Botvid and tell him that we know his plan. If necessary we must fight the crew."

"No, that is exactly what we must not do. We have one big advantage and that is that he does not know we have discovered his plan. I think we must pretend that all is well. We must do exactly as he tells us."

"What, and just accept it when he is cruel to the others? Because as you must have noticed he is getting worse every day!"

Ahl was referring to when, earlier in the day, Botvid shouted and swore at the rowers for, in his opinion, being lazy. He also taunted Anneka about the accident the day before. Even his own son was suffering from the cruelty of the captain; several times they had seen him slap the boy when he did not work fast enough.

"Yes, we have to play along with him. We must wait for our chance to overpower the crew."

"And when would that be?"

"When we are sure that we know where the Jomsviking are."

"I don't know, I think that we should discuss it with the others."

"No, no you can't do that, or the word will eventually get to Ragnar that we have discovered how we are being tricked."

"But I must talk to Ulf and Sture at least."

"Alright, and you had better include Ingemar. He will be wondering what we plan to do."

It proved impossible for the five young plotters to get together in daytime, without awakening Botvid's suspicions. And so two days later it was agreed they should meet that night. The snores of the three men each night indicated when they were asleep.

The five of them gathered at the front of the hold.

"What's all this about?" whispered Ulf.

"Yes, what's the secret, Ahl?" asked Sture.

"What we are going to tell you has to be kept between us. Do we have your word of honour?"

"Yes, let Thor slay me with his hammer if I say anything," said Sture.

"And may Hugin and Munin peck my eyes out if I break my oath," added Ulf. "But what is it?"

"We have been tricked and betrayed."

"Who by?" demanded Ulf.

"Shh, keep your voice down."

One of the snorers stopped and in the dim light the plotters pressed themselves down as low as they could as one of the crew sat up and looked around. They waited for what seemed an eternity before the man lay down again and resumed his snoring.

"Ingemar will tell you what he heard the first morning of the voyage – go on, tell them," said Ahl.

When the boy had finished his story, there was a shocked silence for a few moments as Ulf and Sture considered what to say. Before they could speak, Ingir spoke.

"We expect that the Jomsviking are waiting somewhere for us to catch up with them, then Botvid will hand us over."

"But before he can do that we must act," said Ulf.

"Yes, this is true. But remember why we are here. We are trying to save our families."

Ingir interrupted Ahl and said, "So we want Botvid to lead us to them."

"And then we overpower the crew," suggested Sture.

"Yes, but the question is, how?"

"There are twenty of us," said Sture.

"But they are armed!" Ulf exclaimed.

"Shh, Ahl and I will work out a plan and we

will meet you again tomorrow night to tell you."

"Alright, Ingir, tomorrow night we meet again," said Sture.

"And remember, not a word to anyone."

"You have our word, Ahl."

With that the five teenagers returned to their sleeping places, all now tormented by the thought that they too could end up with a slave collar round their necks in the market at Miklagård.

The following night the plotters met again. Ulf and Sture had had time to think about the situation and had all sorts of fanciful ideas about overpowering the crew and taking command of the vessel. Ingir and Ahl listened to them patiently before explaining their plan.

"First of all, if we are to take over the ship we have to know how to sail it. Sture and Ulf, we want you to watch the way the crew work and learn from them. Agreed?"

The two boys assented to Ingir's idea.

Then Ahl explained how they were going to seize control when the time came.

"We expect that when we get near to the Jomsviking fleet, Botvid will try to trick us in some way. He knows he will need help to get us all into the hands of the Jomsviking. He does not want us to resist – we are too valuable to him for us to be injured. We expect that he will try to get a message to them to come and help him. When we think this is going to happen we must take over the ship."

"But how?" asked Ingemar.

"By disabling the crew, not by force but another way."

"What other way?" asked Ulf loudly.

There was a grunt and a curse and they saw the silhouette of Botvid crawling out of his sleeping fur.

He roared out, "What in the name of the gods is going on? Who is talking at this time of night! Shut up, shut up, you lousy curs or I will thrash you."

Several of the sleeping children were woken and there was a general hubbub as people asked what was going on. The five plotters took the opportunity of the confusion to creep back to their places.

Chapter 11

The Plan is Hatched

After the incident which interrupted their secret meeting, Ahl and Ingir were much more careful about gathering together with their co-conspirators. In fact, they were not able to meet again before matters became very serious. The brother and sister noticed that they were being watched very closely by Botvid and sometimes the other crew members. Ragnar had obviously been told by his father to keep close to Ahl and Ingir and very annoyingly he always found his way to them when they had a break from chores.

Ahl and Ingir were sitting on some rocks with Anneka and Ingemar eating their supper when Ragnar first came across to join them. Before he reached them Ingir hissed in Ahl's ear, "Now be nice to him, he mustn't guess that we suspect him." Ahl let out a quiet groan, but did as Ingir suggested.

Eventually, they found it easier for one of them to engage Ragnar in conversation while the other tried to get some minutes with Sture and Ulf.

Their journey continued in reasonable weather

and they made good progress east, but there was no sign of the Jomsviking. They saw the occasional small fishing boat, but no Viking vessels.

Then on the sixth day the wind increased and they had their first experience of how angry the sea could be. The ship rolled and pitched so alarmingly that they all had to hold onto their thwarts to avoid being thrown overboard. It was not long before some of the boys and girls started to feel ill and soon several were hanging precariously over the side being sick.

Those who were less affected helped the others. It was while she was doing this that Ingir, who did not feel too bad, got her idea, an idea of how to overpower the captain and his men. Ragnar was unwell and for once the brother and sister could speak to each other without being listened to.

"Ahl, you see how helpless our sick friends are? We have to make Botvid and his men just as helpless."

"But how?"

They were interrupted by a shout from the captain: "Ahl, help Grim to lower the sail, the wind is getting too strong. We will row into the lee of that island over there and rest for the night."

Soon the ship was tied up in a sheltered bay and the cooks were lighting a fire.

"Where are you going, Ingir?" called Ragnar as Ingir wandered through the low undergrowth between the trees.

"To look for berries – there are lots here."

Ragnar had obviously decided that this was not an activity he wanted to take part in and instead sat down beside Ahl. But Ingir had not told the whole truth, for while she was looking for berries, she was also trying to find something else. When she returned from her walk she handed out berries to those near her from a wooden cup in her left pocket, but what she had in her right pocket she kept secret.

Each evening over the next few days when they made landfall, by keeping Ragnar occupied, two or three of the five were able to snatch a conversation together. By their ninth day at sea, the plan was ready and the ringleaders knew their roles. This was just as well, as the very next day Botvid called Ahl to the stern to talk to him.

"We will soon be at an island called Sand Harbour where I know that the Jomsviking often gather before they leave to go south to Wollin or across the sea, east, to Novgorod."

Ahl had to pretend that all was well. He said, "Is there anywhere nearby where we can hide to prepare an attack?"

"You're a bright lad aren't you? That is precisely what I had in mind. There is a small island called the Skull on the far side of Sand Harbour."

"Why is it called Skull Island?"

"Because the shape of the hill in the middle of the island looks like a skull. We can land there on the side of the island where we can't be seen. There you can prepare your plan of attack."

"How far is Skull Island from Sand Harbour?"

"Only about two hundred paces, very close indeed. I could swim there," he joked.

Ahl humoured the captain by asking, "How do you think we should rescue the captives?"

Botvid sat back, scratched the stubble on his face and grinned his sneering smile. "You are the son of the chieftain, you will have to decide that. If it were my choice, what I would do is to land on Sand Harbour at night. Then, while the Jomsviking are sleeping, I'd steal their boats and sail home with the captives."

Ahl, for all his inexperience, realised this plan could not work. The Jomsviking would be warned by Botvid that they were coming. They would walk straight into the arms of their enemy and all be captured. The young warriors could not overcome the Vikings by force. In fact, over the last few days he and Ingir had agreed between them that their whole venture was foolhardy. Twenty young people had no chance against boatloads of hardened fighters. They had been tricked into thinking that it was possible. They now knew that their only chance of recovering any of the captives was if they found one ship which had been separated from the rest. Then the odds would be more in their favour. Ahl decided that he would have to humour Botvid.

"Captain, that sounds like a good idea. So let's make for Skull Island."

The next day was misty, but Botvid was a good navigator and in the middle of the afternoon the ship pulled into a bay similar to the ones they had previously stopped at. However, Ahl and his friends were surprised to see that there were two small shacks on the shore and some people fishing with a net.

Ahl moved to the back of the ship and said to Botvid, "You didn't say that people lived on the island."

The captain growled back at him, "Can't see that it is a matter of concern."

"But they might betray us to the Jomsviking."

Botvid hesitated for a moment seeking an answer, then said, "My men will see that the fishermen don't talk."

Ahl was not satisfied with the answer, but said nothing and returned to his place. He recalled the warning which Ingemar had given him that if he and Ingir made any difficulties they would be thrown to the fishes.

As Botvid had said, the place where they had anchored could not be seen from Sand Harbour. They all went ashore and collected wood to make a cooking fire. There was no danger that the smoke from their fire might attract the attention of the Jomsviking as the fishermen had a fire too and probably did regularly.

While the cooks were preparing the food, Botvid called Ahl over to him.

"Tomorrow morning, Grim and I will take the ship across to Sand Harbour to see if the Jomsviking fleet is there."

"But surely they will see you and suspect something."

The captain had expected this remark and had prepared his reply. "We will land on the opposite side of the island from the harbour and climb up on the hill. From there we will have a good view of the anchorage."

"What about us?"

"You can come with us if you like, but the others will have to wait here."

Ahl did not prolong the conversation; he knew that he must talk to Ingir as soon as possible. He found her helping the cooks.

"Botvid is taking the ship to Sand Harbour tomorrow with just Grim on board. I am certain that he is going to make contact with the kidnappers and get help to capture all of us."

"That's it then, put our plan into action. You had better tell Ulf, Ingemar and Sture as quickly as possible."

"Here comes Ragnar."

"I will keep him busy; I'll ask him to get some more firewood. Hurry, before he gets here."

There was a loud shout from the ship: "Hurry up with the food, we are hungry."

"It will soon be ready, Captain. I will send Ragnar over to you with a pot full of porridge for you and your men," called Ingir.

She glanced around to make sure that no one was watching and then reached into her right pocket. She dropped the contents of her hand into the pot of porridge which she was going to give Ragnar, then she stirred the pot vigorously.

"Ragnar, can you take this porridge to your father and his men please?"

Grim leaned over the side of the ship and lifted the pot which the boy held up to him.

The captain told Ragnar to climb into the ship because he wanted to talk to him. While he was doing so, Grim and the slave gobbled down their porridge. Father and son finished their conversation and Botvid picked up his bowl. He took one mouthful and shouted, "This porridge is foul tasting, damn you! Have these brats not learned to cook after all these days?"

He threw the bowl over the side of the ship and said, "I'm coming ashore to see how you are making it."

He clambered over the side of the ship and waded to the beach.

"What are you fools doing here?" he demanded. "Give me another plate."

Ingir ladled out some porridge which was waiting for the young crew from the big pot on the fire.

Botvid took some on his wooden spoon and blew on it to cool it. He then tasted it. "That's better, give me more."

Ingir looked up and caught Sture's eye. He looked despairingly at her; only Ahl, Ingemar and Ulf knew why.

After this confrontation the atmosphere calmed down. Botvid returned to the ship. Later, when they had all eaten, the others did likewise and prepared to spend the night on board. Gradually, one after another they fell asleep.

It was just after dawn that the sleepers were first disturbed by the sound of moaning. The five conspirators had been anxiously awaiting the outcome of Ingir mixing the finely chopped red-cap mushroom into the porridge given to the crew. She knew that the agaric mushroom was poisonous, and while in small doses it was not deadly, the amount she had used would cause violent stomach pains, sickness and sweating – the crew would be disabled.

Grim and Slav were sitting holding their stomachs and wailing with pain. This was the sign for the boys to act. Sture and Ulf both had lengths of rope coiled up beside them while they had slept. They quickly moved back to where the two sick crew were sitting and threw a rope around each of them from the back, pinioning their arms while they tied them up. Sture seized Grim's knife.

As soon as they started to do this, Ingir stood up and shouted to the young crew, "We have been tricked – Botvid is going to hand us over to the Jomsviking. Help us to overpower the crew."

While she was shouting, Ahl leapt from his place, took *Defender* in hand and held it high in the air over a bemused Botvid, who was still sitting on his bed furs. "Move and you die, you cursed traitor."

The captain looked up and realised that Ahl meant what he said. He glanced over to where Ragnar slept to see if he might help his father and saw that Ingemar was standing over his son with an axe.

There was confusion among the young crew and many questions were being shouted at Ahl and Ingir. She was standing on her thwart and held up her hands to try to quieten her friends.

"We discovered that Botvid and Ragnar have betrayed us. They were going to hand us over to become slaves. We couldn't tell you before because Ragnar, who was the traitor in the cave, would have told his father."

There were insults shouted at Ragnar and cries of support for Ingir and Ahl. Ragnar was tied up and blindfolded like the other two crew members.

As the crowd quietened down, Ruric shouted, "So what are we going to do now?"

"Yes, I thought we were going to attack the Jomsviking and rescue our families?" called Oleg.

Ahl was getting concerned – he was still holding his sword over Botvid, but the big man had twice tried to wriggle away from danger.

"Stop shouting and come to help me, Ruric and Oleg. Quick, grab one of those ropes and tie his hands."

But Botvid, who had not eaten any of the poisoned porridge, was still fit and strong and struggled as the lads tried to tie him. Ahl moved the sword to the man's throat and said, "Stay still, betrayer, or *Defender* will take our revenge."

Eventually, all three crew and Ragnar were bound up and made to sit at the stern of the boat.

"So what are we going to do with them now?" asked Sture.

"Yes, and what about our families?" said Bodil.

Many other voices were raised, asking questions and demanding answers.

"Wait, wait! Listen to me, first we have to make sure that the Jomsviking don't find out that we are here. So we have to make sure that Botvid and his crew can't forewarn them."

"How are we to do that?" shouted Oleg.

"We leave them on this island," said Ahl. "They can fish like the others here."

There was laughter and shouts of approval from the young crew.

Ahl continued, "We will leave them on the shore tied up and throw them a knife as we leave so that they can cut themselves free."

"That's more than they would have done for us," added Ingir.

As the attention of the crowd was held by the speakers, no one noticed that Botvid was gradually working his hands free of the rope which held him.

When Ahl turned round to check on the prisoners, he saw Botvid kick off his sea boots and jump up onto the side of the boat. He turned and shouted, "I'll get you all to the slave market yet!"

As he shouted he jumped into the sea and started swimming towards Sand Harbour. The young people looked on aghast. There was no way they could stop him and they understood that he would betray their presence to the Jomsviking.

Chapter 12

Revenge

Two snakes were basking in the late September sunshine on a rock ledge on the seashore of Sand Harbour. They were dark grey with a black double zigzag pattern on their backs. While the bite of an adder is not usually deadly, the venom can be very painful. They are usually shy creatures and harmless when left alone. As they lay dozing, coiled beside each other, they paid no attention to the sound of a swimmer nearing the shore, for they were used to the splashing of the waves.

The swimmer, Botvid, had forgotten that he was much younger when he last swam such a distance, and now too he was encumbered by wet clothing. He was desperately tired when he reached the safety of the island. As he put his hand on the ledge to pull himself out of the sea, he was surprised that he felt something round and soft.

First one snake and then the other struck at the creature which had disturbed their slumber. There was a yell from the swimmer as he was bitten. He thrashed about in the water for a brief moment and then disappeared below the surface. Whether it was the shock of the bite which brought on his heart attack, or exhaustion, or indeed a combination of the two, will never be known.

On the ship, all the young crew were gathered along the side, helplessly watching the progress of the fleeing Botvid. As he neared the far shore they realised that their fate was sealed and they were certain to be captured. It was thus with incredible surprise that as he reached the safety of the shore, they saw him throw up his arms, shout, and sink beneath the waves.

At first there was silence, then they started asking each other what had happened. As they did so, Ingir realised that Ragnar could not have seen what had happened to his father. She called out, "Quiet everyone, quiet." As she spoke, she pointed at the blindfolded Ragnar and held her finger to her mouth to indicate silence. Despite the disgust they felt for the boy, he had just lost his father and should be told with some sympathy.

Ahl understood Ingir's feeling and shouted, "Let's get the prisoners ashore, Ragnar too."

With the help of some threats and prods by Defender, Grim, Slav and Ragnar were persuaded to get off the ship. Their hands were still bound so the boys lifted and dragged them over the side and onto the shore.

Ingir whispered to Ahl, "You have to tell Ragnar what has happened to his father."

"Me, why me?"

"Because, well, because you have taken command here."

Ahl was silent for while and then said, "Alright, I'll do it."

He clambered over the bow of the boat and joined the bound prisoners who now had their blindfolds off. He led Ragnar aside and quietly broke the bad news to him. From the boat, Ingir watched and was surprised when Ahl stayed for a long time talking with Ragnar. Eventually, he returned to the boat.

"What did he say, Ahl?"

"He was not very upset – he said that Botvid was not really his father anyway and that he often mistreated him. He seems to be very sorry for betraying us; he was forced to do so because he was afraid of his so-called father. He is more concerned that we have left him with those other two villains."

"Well, we can't keep him on the boat after what he has done."

"Perhaps we should. He has sailed a lot with Botvid; he knows how to steer and how the sail should be set. He could be very useful to us."

"I'm not so sure. Can we trust him?"

"I think so, but I would watch him very carefully."

"Well, discuss it with Sture and Ulf and see what they think."

"I will."

Not long afterwards, in agreement with his friends, Ahl untied Ragnar's hands and brought him back to the boat. There were some surprised faces among the young crew, but everyone was mindful of the fact that the boy had just lost his father, so said nothing.

"Ragnar, we want you to teach us all you know about sailing this craft. You can start now. We want to go across to Sand Harbour."

"Isn't that foolish, Ahl?" said Ingir.

"No, we need to find out how many ships the Jomsviking have and when they leave Sand Harbour."

"How will you do that?"

"If we can anchor where Botvid was going, a few of us can creep up to the top of the hill and watch the fleet on the other side."

"Yes, and then we will see if there is an odd ship which gets left behind which we might try to capture," said Ulf.

"And in any case we need to know when they leave and which direction they go," added Sture.

"So we are all in agreement then?" asked Ahl.

Ingir realised that the boys were determined and gave in.

"Alright, but we must be very careful not to be spotted."

"Of course," said her brother. "I will tell all the others what we have decided. Sture and Ulf, you help Ragnar get the ship ready while I gather the others and explain why we have brought Ragnar back and what we are going to do."

There were many questions and protests from

the other crew when Ahl announced that Ragnar was to be forgiven and join them, but Ahl was firm and said that the decision had been made and had to be accepted. He then explained that they were going to take the boat across to Sand Harbour to spy on their enemy.

"Everyone to their oars then, and get ready to row across. Ragnar, you take the steering oar and Sture and Ulf prepare to pull up the anchor. Anneka and Bodil, you pull in the bow line when I say."

Ahl walked to the stern of the ship and pulled out two canvas bags. One was Grim's and the other Slav's. He looked inside them and sure enough there was a knife in Grim's bag. He walked to the bow and threw the two bags onto the shore, close to where the two men were still bound up.

"Here are your sea bags, you two villains. Sture, can you throw Grim's knife onto the shore, so that they can cut themselves free after we have left."

Sture stood at the bow and tossed the knife onto the sand some distance from where the two men were sitting.

Ahl turned and shouted, "Pull up the anchor, boys. Anneka let go the bow."

The short journey across only took a few minutes and then they reversed the process and tied up the ship.

They did not dare to light a fire, so in the late afternoon they had a meal of salted fish, cheese and some fruit. After they had all eaten, Ahl called the crew together. He stood on a rock and in a loud voice said, "From what we heard Botvid say, it seems that your families are being held captive on the other side of this island."

There were shouts of, "Let's go and rescue them then," and, "What are we waiting for?"

Ahl held up his hand and called out, "Think about it – we are twenty young people, we are not trained as warriors and we have very few weapons. We cannot overcome the Jomsviking by fighting them, we must be cleverer."

"What are we going to do then?" shouted Ruric.

"First, we have to find out if our enemies are really on the other side of this hill and where the captives are. Ingir, Sture, Ulf and I will go ashore this evening, climb the hill and see what is happening on the other side."

"What are we going to do if they are there?" shouted Oleg.

"Then we have to find a way to use the only weapon we have."

"What's that?"

"That, Oleg, is surprise. They don't know we are here, even less that Captain Botvid and his crew are not going to deliver us to them."

There was a buzz of conversation between the listeners and then Ahl spoke again. "Everyone must be ready for us to leave very quickly if we are seen. But now, we four are going off to spy on the Jomsviking."

During the last few days, Ahl, Sture, Ingir and

Ulf had gone through a lot of action and worry together and their friendship had strengthened. While Ahl was accepted as their leader, their respect and loyalty for each other had increased. While most of their fellow crew were brave and willing to face the dangers ahead of them, they were the ones whom the others depended upon for leadership.

Later, the four friends reached the top of the hill and found a high rock from which they could see ships in the small harbour. They crouched down and watched the activity in the bay. There were at least fifteen ships and two small rowing boats on the beach. Some of the fleet were pulled up on the shore, but five of the ships were anchored off shore. Even at the distance they were, the young spies could see that there were men and women bound up on these five ships.

"They have kept the captives off the land so that there is no chance of them escaping," whispered Sture to the others. "They are so sure they cannot escape that there are no guards on those ships – all the Jomsviking are ashore."

"And look at that huge ship, the one with all the carvings on the bow and stern – it must be the leader's," said Ingir. She pointed out a vessel pulled up on the shore which had mystical figures all over the hull and figureheads on the front and back. It was painted red and blue with a yellow wavy line along the side.

"If only we could get to those ships which are afloat, we could free the prisoners."

"But how, Ingir?" said Ahl. He turned to the others and said, "Let's get back to our ship and think about a way to do it."

They retraced their steps and boarded the ship. Later, they got together and worked out a plan. It was inspired by the way Sten, their father, had defeated the Jomsviking. Preparations were made and the crew was informed about what was expected of them.

Ahl took Ruric and Ingemar aside and said, "We can't afford to take any chances. You will stay on board the ship and keep Ragnar with you. Don't let him out of your sight. I still feel a bit uneasy about him."

"Don't worry, I'll take care of him if he tries anything," said Ruric with glee.

"I don't want you to bully him, just make sure he does not try to leave the ship."

"Alright then, but if he tries anything he will be sorry."

"And make sure that Ingemar does not fall asleep."

"I'll give him a kick once in a while."

Ahl stood by the side of the boat looking at the rising moon. A few slight ripples caused its reflection in the almost-still water to shimmer and bounce. On shore the huge rounded rocks looked like the backs of giant bears. Ahl knew that rounded side of the boulders faced north; his father had taught him that this was the way that the gods had created the land. The rougher side of the rocks were on the southern side. The moon was rising in the east, so as he looked at it he knew that he had his back to the west, the direction of Birka and the way they would have to travel to go home.

He was nervous. For the first time they were on the ship, far from home, with no adults. Everything depended on the decisions he and Ingir made with their friends. He gazed at the silhouette of the fir trees on a piece of land jutting out into the sea, under where the moon was making its steady ascent. Suddenly he became aware of some movement on the shore, then there was a splash. He stared into the darkness, trying to make out the source of the noise.

Sture was at his side and said, "It must have been a sea otter or a seal."

"There would have been a bigger splash if a man had jumped or fallen in," added Ulf.

The three of them listened intently for a while and, satisfied that they did not have human company on the shore, they tried to relax.

"All ready then?" asked Ahl in a quiet voice.

There were whispers of assent from the others.

"Ingir, are you sure you have the flint?"

"Yes, and Bodil has the tar."

"Do you have the knives?"

"Yes, three."

They had taken all the knives they could find on their boat and shared them out.

Ahl turned and said, "Ruric, you know what to do. You, Ragnar and Ingemar must have the boat all ready for us to escape quickly when we return."

"I'll make sure they do their work."

Six of them – the four close friends with Bodil and Anneka – clambered over the side of the ship and dropped into the shallow water below. They made their way over the smooth rocks and headed single file into the forest beyond. Sture was in front of the column as they pushed their way through the dense branches and up the hill.

After a few moments they heard the crack of twigs and then the crash of some heavy object forcing its way through the bushes in front of them. The young warriors stopped, and whispered to each other. "What was that? Have we been discovered? What shall we do?"

Sture turned to Ulf behind him and hissed, "It must have been an elk which we disturbed. Come on, follow me."

Ulf turned to Ahl behind him and said, "Tell the others it was an elk."

It was not easy to walk quietly as they laboured up the hill. Their progress was slow as they tried to avoid the many dead branches and twigs which cracked loudly as they trod on them. A light rain started falling and the rocks and boulders became slippery, adding to the difficulties. At last they reached the clearing at the top and were able to look down on the Jomsviking camp below. The night was lit by several fires on the beach. Groups of Viking warriors sat around the fires laughing, shouting and drinking from horns. By the flickering firelight it was just possible to make out the shape of the ships moored off shore, as well as those pulled up on land.

The watchers on the hill gathered together and Ahl addressed them.

"You see the big ship on the far side? We think that is their leader's ship. It's the one we will set fire to. But, Ingir, before you do so, make sure there are no prisoners aboard."

"Of course," she replied.

"Then let's go."

Chapter 13

Action!

They walked down the hill as quietly as they could and in darkness continued towards the far end of the Viking camp. When they reached it, Ahl whispered, "Good luck, girls," as they disappeared towards the ship which was to be their target.

The three boys crouched, hiding behind one of the rowing boats. Every now and again they peered over the boat to see if they could see any sign of what the girls were doing. They waited for what seemed to be a very long time and then Sture whispered to the others, "Something must have gone wrong, it is taking too—"

Before he could finish the sentence there was a whoosh and a bright flash as flames, fuelled by the tar, soared into the air from one of the ships, the huge vessel they had seen earlier. This was the signal for the boys to act. As the Vikings around the campfires rushed towards the burning ship, the boys pushed one of their rowing boats into the sea. Ulf jumped in and started to row towards the three girls who were swimming away from the blaze they had started. His task was to rescue them.

Ahl and Sture pushed the other boat out, jumped in and Ahl grabbed the oars. He pulled with all his strength towards the nearest of the ships which were at anchor and very soon reached it. Sture climbed aboard and by the light of the flames started to cut the ropes which were holding the prisoners. When several were freed, he shouted, "Raise the sail and up with the anchor, quickly." The prisoners who had been liberated rushed around doing as requested. Sture then jumped back into the rowing boat and they rowed to the next ship to do the same thing. By this time, Ulf with the three girls was also trying to find the prison ships in the dark. He pulled at the oars as hard as he could and came up alongside one ship at anchor. The girls climbed aboard and cut the ropes holding the prisoners, leaving a knife on board.

Ulf shouted out to the freed prisoners, "Remember, head west, keep the rising sun behind you."

The warriors on the shore had by this time realised they had been tricked, but they could not easily do anything because the two rowing boats had gone. Several of them started to prepare their beached ships to go to sea, but in the dark this took time and, meanwhile, several of the ships with the prisoners had disappeared into the night. The situation was made worse for the Vikings as the flames from the big ship were spreading to other vessels.

Ulf decided that the girls, who were wet through and now very cold, had done enough. He rowed ashore and let them run off into the darkness to get back to their ship. Then he turned and rowed out again to try to help Ahl and Sture. He did not know that they had finished their task and had already beached their boat, making the most of the dark and confusion to get away.

Sture and Ahl had come ashore at the dark end of the sandy beach and had immediately started to run up the hill. It was very difficult in the dark – they tripped on bushes, banged into trees and slipped on rocks. But after a while they realised they had not been seen and no one was following them. They slowed down and tried to catch their breath.

Ahl was still puffing when he asked Sture, "Did you see Ulf come ashore with the girls?"

"No, they may be ahead of us. I hope so."

"Come on, we must hurry."

But Ulf was not ahead of them, only the girls were.

As Ulf was rowing to the shore, he became aware of people splashing in the water around the boat. He suddenly realised that several of the Vikings who could swim were surrounding him. The light from the blazing ships was so bright that they had spotted him making towards the shore. Ulf desperately tried to evade the swimmers, but he felt the boat rock as a hand grabbed one side of it. This slowed him down and before long he was being dragged ashore by several swimmers. They were shouting and cursing him as the boat grounded on the sand. Several of them grabbed him and threw him onto the beach. He was sure that he was about to be murdered when there was a loud shout and the commander of the Jomsviking pushed his way through the crowd attacking Ulf. The man grabbed Ulf's jacket and dragged him to his feet. It was too dark to see what the man looked like, but there was no doubt he was extremely big and very angry. The boy was terrified – he was a prisoner of the Jomsviking.

Ahl and Sture slipped and slid their way down the far side of the hill to where their crew had the ship ready to depart. The two of them waded out and climbed aboard.

"Are Ulf and the girls here yet?" asked Ahl.

"The girls are, they're getting some dry clothes, but no sign of Ulf. How did you get on?" shouted Ruric.

"We think we have freed all the prisoners. Their ships are heading west under the cover of darkness; we should join them as quickly as possible so that we can help them to get home."

"But, Ahl, we can't go until Ulf gets here," said Sture.

"No of course not, but we really have to hurry to take advantage of the dark to escape. The Jomsviking are certain to search for us."

There was silence as everyone listened to see if they could hear their missing crew member coming down the slope. Ahl was painfully aware of his dilemma. If they did not escape in the dark they might be captured. But he could not leave Ulf behind.

The whole crew grasped the seriousness of the situation and a tense silence fell on the ship. The rain had stopped and the moon was shining brightly. The quiet was only broken by an occasional whisper and the sounds of nature, the movement of the sea and the slap as wavelets lapped against the hull. Occasionally they heard a fish jump, but there was no sound which likened that of someone coming down the hill. They waited and waited. Gradually, there was increasing panic among them that unless they left soon, they might all be captured.

Ahl took Sture aside and said, "This could be a disaster for us. If we all get captured we will pay dearly for what we have done. Yet we have to wait for Ulf to join us."

"We can't, Ahl. We have to leave soon."

"But I can't leave my best friend behind."

"We may have to."

"That would be a horrible thing to do."

"You will have to decide."

There was a silence while Ahl thought. It was a terrible situation. He wondered for a moment what his father would have done. That helped him to make a decision.

He shouted, "Ruric, raise the sail, we will leave now, immediately."

Sture shouted across the ship to Ahl, "But what about—"

"Ulf knew the risks. We cannot chance nineteen of us getting caught by these villains to save one.

"Yes, yes of course. You are right."

Chapter 14

Homeward Bound

With the knowledge they had gained earlier through observing how Botvid sailed his ship and with Ragnar's help, even in the dark the young crew knew exactly what to do, and before long they were taking advantage of a brisk northeasterly wind to head west. But they were doing exactly what Botvid said no one should do in these treacherous waters – they were sailing at night. By the light of the moon they could see where islands were, but they had no way of knowing if there were rocks which might tear the bottom out of their ship. Their new dilemma was that they wanted to escape as fast as possible, but if the ship hit a rock at speed, they would be wrecked.

Ragnar shouted from his position with the steering oar, "Ahl, I must speak with you."

Ahl was sitting alone with his thoughts, feeling very guilty about having left Ulf. He got up and climbed over the thwarts to reach Ragnar. "What is it?"

"We must slow down. I remember when we

came this way that Botvid steered very carefully. There must be shallows around here."

Ahl thought for a moment, balancing the need for speed against the danger Ragnar had expressed.

"What should we do then?"

"We must reef the sail; you know, roll part of it up so that we sail more slowly."

As he spoke there was a grinding sound and the ship stopped suddenly. There were screams and shouts from the frightened crew as the ship lurched over sideways. The ship was stationary for a few seconds and then there was a strong gust of wind. Gradually they started moving again. There were gasps of relief.

"What happened, Ragnar?" asked Ahl.

"We ran aground on a rock, but we were lucky, the wind is gusting and it pushed us off again."

Ahl needed no second bidding; he shouted, "Ruric and Sture, roll up part of the sail to make it smaller."

The two crew members rushed to do as ordered.

Had they known it, they could have sailed very slowly from the start, for the Jomsviking had lost several ships in the fire and were not going to risk wrecking any of the remainder. Despite his fury, the leader of the Vikings had decided he would have to accept the loss of the prisoners. He had other business – his ships were stacked with furs looted from villages they had raided and he wanted to trade these for silver at Novgorod, before returning to their base at Wollin in the south. This had to be done before the winter storms. At least he had one slave to sell, a fine young warrior.

As day broke, the helmsman of the *Orm* got a much better idea of the dangers presented by rocks and islands. Sture was now steering the ship while Ragnar got some sleep. He called out to Ahl, "Can we put someone at the bow of the ship to look out for any dangers?"

Ahl had been dozing, but the call woke him. "Good idea. Bodil, can you go to the front and keep a look out?"

Bodil did as requested. She stood peering forwards looking for any change of colour in the sea which would indicate shallow water. But it was not rocks or shallow water which, after a while, caused her to shout back to Sture.

"Sture, look, over there to the north. It's a ship."

Those who were awake rushed to the starboard side to see what Bodil was pointing at. Sure enough, there was a ship with its sail furled. It seemed motionless and the mast was at a strange angle. Ahl clambered back to where Sture stood and climbed up onto the side of the ship to get a better view.

"It is one of the Jomsviking ships, it must have run aground." By now, everyone was awake and peering at the stricken vessel.

"It must be one of the ships with the freed prisoners," said Sture.

"Ruric, Ragnar, get our sail down. Everyone stand by with your oars."

With the sail lowered, the ship quickly started to slow down.

By now all the crew were awake and ready on their thwarts. Ahl called out to them, "We are going to row across to the other vessel and see if we can help."

As they neared the other ship they began to hear voices shouting out to them and soon they saw faces, faces they recognised, for some of those on the ship stuck on the rocks were parents or brothers and sisters of the crew of the *Orm*.

One of the men on the grounded ship was standing on the bow with a coil of rope. He called out, "Can you try to pull us off the rocks?"

Sture called out to the rowers, "Slow down, row very slowly, we don't want to get caught on the same rocks!"

"Throw us the line," called Ahl.

The man threw the rope, but it fell short and into the sea.

"We will have to get closer," said Ragnar.

Sture realised that he did not have the skill to bring the ship close enough to the other vessel in the strong wind.

"Ragnar, can you take over the helm and guide us closer?" he called.

Ragnar took the steering oar and called instructions to the rowers while he carefully steered close, but not too close, to the rocks. Very slowly they approached the other ship and the man threw the rope again. This time several hands on the *Orm* grabbed at the rope and Oleg managed to catch it.

"Pass the rope along to the stern and we will try

to tow the other ship off," called Ahl.

When this was done, he shouted, "Row as hard as you can, altogether now."

The crew pulled and pulled at their oars and very gradually they could see the stricken ship begin to stand upright and start to follow them.

Once they were in deep water, the two ships came alongside each other. There were many hugs and kisses between the families and relatives on both ships.

Ahl and Ingir sat in the stern watching the celebration. Though nothing was said between them, their happiness at seeing the joyful reunions was tinged with a little sadness, for they had no family to greet.

Ingir said, "Ahl, why should we feel sad, look, Ragnar is also without friends and relations. He is sitting alone; bring him over here."

The three of them sat together watching all the happiness and rejoicing in front of them, but soon their mood changed when the story of the rescue and their part in it was told to the freed prisoners. Many of the adults climbed over the thwarts to shake hands and hug the children of the chieftain and their new friend, Ragnar.

"We must move on in case we are being followed," called Ahl. The adults agreed and returned to their own boat. They let go the lines between them and the two ships drifted apart. *Orm* and the Jomsviking longship both sailed west together and a week later, when they entered the harbour at Birka, they found that the other four ships were already there. On the quay was the familiar figure of the Shaman. He walked to where the *Orm* was being tied up and waited for Ahl and Ingir to step ashore.

"Welcome back to your home, young ones. You have performed a great act and assured yourselves of a place in the history of this island. Come, come, we are to have a special celebration of your achievement."

Ahl looked at the Shaman, who was now surrounded by a crowd of returned islanders. The young warrior raised his hand for silence and said, "The achievement was not only mine but that of the whole crew. Sadly, we have lost a good friend, for Ulf has not returned."

There was a wailing sound in the crowd and Ahl realised that it must be Ulf's mother. Ahl put up his hand again to quell the comments and the compliments and with a loud voice said, "We believe that Ulf has been captured by the Jomsviking and that they have taken him to Novgorod. I make this promise – when the snows have melted after the winter and the geese return from the southern lands, I will go in search of my friend and save him from slavery."

When he raised *Defender* in the air there were cheers from the crowd and then they all set off for the celebration feast. As they did so, Sture and Ingir and some of the others grabbed Ahl by the sleeve and said, "If you go east in the spring, you will not be alone."

Epilogue

The only light in the room came from the dying fire, though outside the full moon illuminated the firs and pines surrounding the cottage.

"The fire is low, can someone put a log on before it goes out?" said the old man. "And all this talking has made me thirsty. Bring me an ale, if you please."

One of the young listeners threw a log on the fire and another went over to the barrel on the table and filled a horn with a drink for the speaker.

"Thank you, young lad. So that is my story, or at least, the beginning of it."

"But what happened to Ulf?" asked one.

"Ah, that's another long story – you'll have to come to see me another day to hear it."

"Why did you make friends with Ragnar when he was so treacherous?" asked someone else.

"Well, there's good and bad in everyone, sometimes it takes a while to discover the good."

"Did the Jomsviking come back again?"

"Enough, enough questions. Come and see me

another evening and I will tell you more. Now off you go to your homes."

The old man slowly stood up, walked across to the door and opened it. The listeners reluctantly got up and filed through, out into the moonlight.

"Goodnight. Come back next full moon and I will tell you more."

The old man went back into the house and sat before the now blazing log. He closed his eyes and the memories came flooding back to him.

Glossary

Anguish – distress.
Bemused – confused.
Burly – muscular, strong.
Cavern – large cave.
Chores – tasks, jobs.
Cur – an unkind way to describe a dog.
Despicable – wicked, shameful.
Encumbered – weighed down.
Esteem – respect.
Fugitive – a runaway.
Funereal – the ship carrying the Chieftain's ashes.
Furtive – secretive.
Gruff – bad-tempered, grumpy.
Helm – the control to steer a ship.
Hubbub – noise, din.
Imbecile – someone who is completely mad and useless.
Impetuous – hasty in making decisions or doing things.
Imps – little elves or fairies.
Jomsviking – a very aggressive band of Vikings

based on an island in the south Baltic sea.

Lee – protected from the wind.

Looting – robbing.

Miklagård – the Viking name for what is now Istanbul.

Oath of allegiance – a promise of loyalty.

Pall (of smoke) – a column.

Perplexed – puzzled, confused or mystified.

Plummeted – dropped, plunged.

Pommel – the end of a sword handle.

Rapt – attentive, very interested.

Red ochre – a red colour which comes from iron, similar to rust.

Resentment – anger, bitterness.

Ritual – a traditional ceremony, usually religious.

Rite – part of a ritual.

Scabbard – a case or covering for a sword or knife.

Shaman – a holy man with magical power.

Shrine – a holy place or monument.

Silhouette – outline shape.

Staves – the strips of wood to make a barrel.

Subterfuge – a scheme to fool someone.

Tar – an inflammable sticky thick black liquid Vikings made from pine roots to waterproof their ships. Today used to make roads.

Treacherous – (here) disloyal, unfaithful.

Urn – a pot or container.

Valhalla – the place where warriors, killed in battle, went after death.

Vanquished – beaten, defeated.

Venom – poison.

Next in the Series

Children of the Chieftain: Banished

The boys climbed up one side of the wooden fence, balanced on the top and then jumped down the other side into the long undergrowth. The spiky bushes clung to their trousers and they had to struggle to free themselves from the dense vegetation.

"Look there's the path to the harbour. Come on, hurry, we might find a fishing boat to escape in," said Ahl.

"And if there isn't one, what do we do then, Ahl?"

"Shut up, Ruric, save your breath for running," said Sture, the third member of the trio.

Ahl reached the path first and stood impatiently waiting for the other two.

"Come on, come on. We have a chance if we can outrun them. They are wearing heavy armour."

As the other two reached the path they heard a curse shouted from behind them. They looked round and saw the head of a warrior peering over the fence.

"Quick, quick, they have seen us," said Ahl,

waving at the other two to hurry them up.

"Shall we drop our weapons and shields, Ahl? We can run faster without them."

"No, no, Ruric, we may need them."

The three of them started to run as fast as the weight of their equipment would allow them, occasionally glancing back to see how close their pursuers were. Ahl was right, they were outrunning the men.

Minutes later, panting for breath, they arrived at the harbour. They ran up and down the quay seeking a boat of any description in which they could escape, but there was not a single craft to be had.

"By the gods, I can see all the boats! The fishermen are out on the lake," wailed Ruric, pointing out to the bay.

The boys looked around frantically, where could they go to avoid the men? The harbour was on a narrow strip of land which stretched into the lake. There was water on three sides. They were trapped!

"What now, Ahl?"

"We must fight them, Sture."

"Fight them? They are huge and better armed than we are."

"We have no choice, Ruric, unless you want to learn to swim."

The three of them turned and stood side by side watching the two men, who were some way ahead of a large group of warriors, getting closer and closer to them. When the two armoured fighters realised that the boys were trapped, they stopped trotting and slowly walked along the strip of land leading to the quay where the teenagers were standing.

Breathing heavily from the exertion of running, the two powerful men taunted the boys as they advanced towards them. One was slightly taller than the other and had a beard. The shorter man had a moustache which almost reached his chin. Each of the men wore a chain mail shirt which was gathered at the waist by a belt on which hung a long dagger in a leather sheath. The middle of their faces could not be seen as they had long metal nose protectors which were part of the round helmets they wore. There was no doubt however that their faces were full of hate and disdain for the three in front of them. As they came forward about two paces apart from one another, they raised their swords in their right hands and beat them rhythmically against the shields they held in their left. They added to the sound of this beating by howling loudly at the boys.

The trapped trio raised their own shields, readying them for protection from the onslaught that was about to come, and grasped their weapons even more tightly.

Although Ruric was the biggest of the boys, he started to whimper with terror as it became clear that there was no escape for them. They would have to face their adversaries.

"Shut up, Ruric. Remember what we have learnt. We must take them by surprise."

"Surprise! How can we surprise them, Ahl? They are upon us!"

For more information about the author and his work
visit www.michaelwills.eu

Lightning Source UK Ltd.
Milton Keynes UK
UKHW041516030419
340420UK00001B/7/P